D0595320

Taking Care of Yoki

Barbara Campbell

Taking Care of Yoki

HarperTrophy
A Division of HarperCollinsPublishers

Library of Congress Catalog Card Number: 85-46040
ISBN 0-06-440173-1 (pbk.)

First Harper Trophy edition, 1986.

A Scott Foresman Edition
ISBN 0-673-80134-9

Printed in the U.K.

TO MY SONS,
Jonathan and Zachary

ACKNOWLEDGMENTS

To my mother for the fun we had recalling old songs and marveling at what small things we remembered and important things we had forgotten.

And to Mrs. Evelyn Watkins Clay, an outstanding and unforgettable St. Louis elementary school teacher, whose innovative instruction and compassion many years ago has had lasting impact on my creative and intellectual development.

CONTENTS

1

A HORSE CALLED YOKI

The streetcar screeches to a stop on the corner near :1 my house, and the noise is so loud that everybody riding puts their fingers in their ears. Some lady sitting behind me says, "They ought to put oil on those wheels and rails. That's enough noise to blow your ears off."

I jump up and run to the back to get off. I just get started down the steps when Chuckie Williams pushes ahead of me and knocks my lunch bucket out of my hands. The bucket goes *clang, clatter* down the steps, and a piece of sweet-potato pie I've been saving just flies out and hits the sidewalk.

"Whatchoo in such a hurry for, Chuckie!" I scream at him, scooping up that squashed-up piece of pie and putting it back in my lunch bucket. "You saw me getting off the streetcar!"

"Ain't seen a thing." He laughs and keeps on running up the sidewalk, dragging his raggedy knapsack behind him. "And if I did, whatchoo goin' to do about it?"

"You just watch out for what I'm going to do about it. Water start running uphill, it'll be so bad!"

He laughs some more at that and keeps on moving.

I don't understand people like Chuckie. He does mean and nasty things just to be doing them. Me, when I do something mean, it's for a good reason.

When I get to the corner of my block, Culpepper Street, I forget all about Chuckie, such a delicious smell is coming out of Jenkins's Bake Shop.

Everybody calls it a bake shop, but Mr. Jenkins doesn't just sell cookies and cake. Some days he doesn't sell any because it's hard to get enough butter, eggs, and sugar now that the war is on. I guess most of the food has to be sent to the soldiers fighting in the war so they won't starve.

So Mr. Jenkins has to sell other things in his bakery, like the smoked pigs' feet, tails, and knuckles hanging on hooks in the window. Lucky for me they sell good things in the bake shop too, like red and black jelly candy that look like buttons, sour pickles, and malt balls.

As I pass by, Mr. Jenkins sticks his head out the front door and says, "Hey, you, Bob, Miz Jenkins say come on in out the cold a minute. She got somethin' for ya."

I do a double skip and turn around. The only thing that something could be is something good.

Mr. Jenkins holds the door open for me to come in, and then he goes out to a truck that just parked in front of the shop.

"Hi, Mrs. Jenkins," I say.

She is standing behind the counter wrapping up three cream puffs.

"Hi, Barbara Ann, puddin'," she says, looking up and smiling. She and my teacher at school and the lady who lives upstairs in our rooming house are the only ones to call me by my real name. Everybody else calls me Bob or the nickname to that, Bobby, since I can remember. I guess to some people I look like a Barbara and to others like a Bob or a Bobby.

"I thought I'd give you and your mama and your grandmama somethin' sweet to eat · after supper tonight."

"They sure look good, Mrs. Jenkins," I say. My mouth is watering and my stomach begins to growl, I'm so hungry.

"Sorry just a shake a powdered sugar on 'em. Sugar's hard to come by 'cause of this war. Ain't right a cream puff got such a litta bit of sugar on it. A real cream puff need to look like it's covered with snow," she says, putting them into my lunch bucket.

"That's all right, Mrs. Jenkins," I say. "Maybe the war will be over soon. Maybe next month."

"Next month ain't hardly going to come, the war be over," she says.

"I hope it will, because I can't wait much longer."

"You'll wait like everybody else waits. Can't do nothin' but wait," she says.

My eyes begin to well up, and I'm surprised that I feel like crying that bad. I guess I can't stand to hear Mrs. Jenkins telling me that the war is not going to be over and that I *have* to wait. One thing I hate is doing what everybody else does and another is having to do something I don't want to do and the worst is hearing somebody tell me that.

"Maybe I'm not like everybody else," I say. "I need this war to be over so my daddy can come home and so everything can go back to normal."

"Now, don't everybody want that. But wantin' ain't gettin'."

Mrs. Jenkins is making me tired with that kind of talk. "Maybe the news will say that the war is over. It's possible."

"And then what'll happen?"

"When my daddy comes home, I'll take him off somewhere so we can be by ourselves and I'll tell him what's been bothering me, and I know he'll know what to do about it."

"Can't your mother and your grandmama help you? Just in case the war ain't over tomorrow?"

"Everybody got a way that they help. I just need the :5 way my daddy can help. That's all."

"What's botherin' you so much, you studyin' on your daddy comin' home so bad?"

"I got a lot of things to make up my mind about, like whether I'm going to be baptized this Easter."

"You eight years old going on nine. 'Bout time you decide. Getting baptized just mean you know right from wrong and you ready to do the right things . . . try, anyway. A lot of people baptized, shouldn't be."

"Sometimes I start out doing what's right, and it turns out wrong. I can't help that. Suppose that happens after I'm baptized . . . you see what I mean?"

"It ain't easy . . ." she says. But just then the bell over the door shaped like a Santa Claus tinkles, and Mr. Jenkins pushes through. He's carrying a whole half a pig slung over his shoulder. The pig is so long, his hoof is slapping against the back of Mr. Jenkins's ankle, and it's cut straight down the middle so you can see its ribs and its bones. The pig's skin is smooth and pink because all the hair is off of it. What a terrible sight!

"Everybody outta the way—comin' through!" Mr. Jenkins says, and he sounds like that pig is heavy.

"Eugene Leonard Jenkins," Mrs. Jenkins says, looking happy, "where did you get all of that pig meat?"

"Tell you in a minute. Got to get this load of pig offa my shoulder first," says Mr. Jenkins, going into the big kitchen in the back where they do all the baking and cooking.

He comes back out wiping the sweat off his forehead with the bottom of his long white apron, and he's smiling.

As for me, I think I'm going to throw up. I can't stand to see dead animals like that. Especially the way they look when they're made ready to eat. It's not natural. When my father used to go hunting down South and bring back rabbits skinned all over except for the head and the tail and feet, I'd always have rice and butter for supper. Nothing else. And by myself. I couldn't stand to sit at the table with that rabbit. Once I saw my grandmother kill a chicken when I went to visit her in the South. She picked out a white hen and grabbed it by the neck and started swinging the chicken around and around until its neck was broken. Everybody had fried chicken and you know what I had— butter and rice.

"Whew!" says Mr. Jenkins, "that was heavy, but it's worth it. I can smoke that pig out back in the smokehouse, have all kinds of meat come Easter. People be lined up around the block, they so happy to get it."

"Where'd it come from?" Mrs. Jenkins asks.

"Black market been my friend again. Truck just drove up," he says, pulling some long sharp knives from behind the meat counter and then going back into the kitchen. "Yes, sir, black market, don't know what we'd do without it."

Everybody is always talking about this black market. But they never say what it really is or where it is. All I know is that it started because of the war. Everybody acts like it's such a big secret. Maybe they act like that because they buy things there that we're not supposed to be able to get because the war is on. I wonder how they find out where the black market is. I've never seen it. I wonder whether it's painted black. I asked my mother once, but she just laughed and said, "You learn about the black, the green, the red market soon enough."

Now, does that make sense?

I say good-bye and thanks to Mr. and Mrs. Jenkins and head out the door.

Next I stop at Yoki's Grocery two stores down from Jenkins's Bake Shop. Yoki's is named after a horse, and that horse is a friend of mine. He pulls the milk-delivery wagon every morning, and after he finishes, he lives out back of the store in a broken-down woodshed.

Every morning Mr. Strausburger, who is the milkman and the grocery man, hitches him up to the milk wagon, and Yoki pulls it up and down the streets, stopping where Mr. Strausburger has to deliver the milk and pick up empty bottles.

Yoki's so smart, he knows all the stops by heart, and Mr. Strausburger never has to say *whoa* the way the cowboys do in the movies. He just clops up to the right house and stops.

Mr. Strausburger is sweeping up some sawdust from the floor when I come in the store.

"Hi, Mr. Strausburger. How's Yoki?"

"Not bad for an old horse," he says. "And that goes for me too."

Then he gives a laugh that sounds like "A-hark, a-hark, a-hark."

"Can I go out back and see him?"

"Well, Bobby, I don't know . . . there's still some ice out there, and it's all rutted . . ."

"Please?"

"Can't hurt nothing, I guess," Mr. Strausburger says. "Be careful you don't slip, though."

I run back past the counter and through the storeroom that's got empty flattened-out cans and bottles of grease Mr. Strausburger collects from everybody to send off to make things for the war, and out the back door.

"Yoki, I'm here," I say as I open the shed and go inside. He is standing on some hay and tied up so he can't run away, I guess. The first thing I always do is untie him. I don't know why I do it. He just stands there like he doesn't know he's untied. But it makes me feel better.

"How you doing, Yoki, boy?" I say, patting his nose. He leans down and gives me a nip, nip on my shoulder.

"You miss me?"

He just stands there and blows through his lips. I'm crazy about this horse. He doesn't remind me of any horse in the movies. He doesn't *clippity, cloppity* fast and his tail doesn't swish. He's very slow, with big hooves that have hair hanging over them. He's got a dip in his back and a little stubby tail. But he's got a beautiful face.

Ever since I read *Black Beauty*, I've thought that he

looks like old broken-down Black Beauty when he was almost worked to death pulling people in a taxi wagon.

But at least when Black Beauty was young, he had a good friend named Merrylegs. I don't think Yoki's ever had a good friend like that, and I bet he's never just run around free in a pasture. That's why I come when I can to keep him company.

"It's cold in here, Yoki. Ain't right you got to live in such a raggedy old house. When my father comes home from the navy, I'm going to ask him to make you a real stable."

He looks at me and blinks his eyes, and then he leans down and pushes against my lunch bucket.

"I don't have anything for you today. No need to push on my lunch bucket, ain't a thing in it for you."

He just pushes harder. "I tried, but nobody had an apple at school today to trade. I brought some delicious sweet-potato pie, and if anybody had had one, you know they would have exchanged their dessert for that. My girl friend Shirley had a sour pickle, and I know you don't like that, and Audrey had a jelly bread sandwich. The teacher had some kind of rice pudding with raisins, and nobody likes that."

Yoki acts like he doesn't hear me and almost pushes my lunch bucket out of my hand.

"You think I'm kidding, don't you? Here, see for yourself," I say, opening my lunch bucket.

"All I have is mashed-up sweet-potato pie and three cream puffs for dinner," I say.

Before I can stop him, he leans down and reaches in

with his mouth and picks up the three cream puffs and chews them up and swallows them with the wax paper still on them!

"Yoki! You greedy horse! Those were for our dessert tonight, and you know you're not supposed to eat things like that. You're going to be one sick horse, and everybody is going to blame me!"

Before I can shut my lunch bucket, he leans in again and eats up the sweet-potato pie too.

"Oh, no, Yoki. I'm in big trouble. How could you do this?"

He just pulls back his lips and shows all of his big yellow-and-brown teeth like he's saying, "It was easy." And then he starts nip, nipping my cheek like he's telling me, "Thanks a lot. That was good."

"How many times I have to tell you I'm trying to stay out of trouble? You know how trouble follows me around. Now look what you've done."

I give him a few more pats and look close into his eyes, but he looks just the same to me. "Mr. Strausburger says you got a weak stomach. How come you don't know that?"

I tie him back up and check him again. I wish I knew how to tell when a horse is sick.

I don't want to tell Mr. Strausburger, so I stand in the storeroom in back of the grocery thinking of what to do. If I don't tell him, Yoki might get sicker and sicker and nobody will know why. If I do, he might not let me see Yoki again.

I'm surprised when I come out of the storeroom. There are a lot of people lined up inside and outside. Mr. Strausburger's so busy waiting on people, he doesn't notice me standing nearby.

"Mr. Strausburger," I say.

"Oh, Bobby, go out front and count the people. See how fast they are lining up. Just got these chickens in. I'm afraid I won't have enough for everybody."

I go to the door and count ten people outside.

"Mr. Strausburger . . . Mr. Strausburger . . ." I say louder. He keeps working. I almost give up and leave, but then I think about Yoki and go behind the counter and grab Mr. Strausburger's apron.

"Now what do you want, young lady," he asks, frowning and holding up a chicken just ready to weigh it.

"I didn't mean for it to happen, Mr. Strausburger, but Yoki just ate three cream puffs with wax paper still on them," I say very fast.

"Now, how did he do that?" he asks me. He doesn't look mad, just like any minute he's going to go "A-hark, a-hark."

"It was a mistake. It just happened," I say, and I can't help it, but my chin is trembling like I'm going to start crying any minute.

"Now, Bobby, don't you worry. Yoki's a strong old horse. The worst he could get is a touch of the colic, and you cure that by walking it off of him. Pulling that milk wagon ought to do it."

"But suppose he gets sicker than that?"

"It's possible, but I don't think so. . . . Now, I got to—"

"What's taking so long!" yells somebody in the back of the line.

"Now, you just be patient," Mr. Strausburger calls out. "Run along, Bobby; your grandmother's going to be worried about ya."

I start to skip the rest of the way home, I feel so good. Yoki's not going to be really sick. But then I stop skipping. What am I going to tell Mama about the cream puffs? Then I start skipping again. I'm just going to tell her the truth. Maybe everything is changing for me. Maybe I won't get in trouble about that, either.

2

THE WEATHER FLAG

When I get almost home, I see our landlady, Mrs. :13
Beene, out front propping up our red and white flag
with the blue star Mother sewed on it.

Everybody got somebody away fighting in the war
puts a flag with a star in the window. If there is more
than one person gone to war, you put more than one
star.

Our house is the only one on the block with a flag in
the front yard. Everybody else's is in a front window.
Ours is different because Mrs. Beene wanted to do it
that way, and it doesn't work, either.

She dug a hole in the ground and she poked the flagpole in it and then put four big rocks around it to hold it up. Every day the flag leans further and further over until it falls down, and then she has to start propping it up all over again.

Some days nobody knows my father is away fighting in the war at all, because when the weather is bad, Mrs. Beene takes the flag in and props it by the door in the hall. But Mother says something good comes out of something bad after all, because anytime we see that the flag is inside, we know it's going to rain or snow. That's why we call it the weather flag. Mother also says she's not going to worry about that flag because she's got too much to be thankful for. We're all thankful because the star on our flag is blue. If it was gold-colored, that means that whoever went to war got killed.

I see puffs of steam coming out of Mrs. Beene's mouth, it's so cold. She picks up her broom when she finishes with the flag and begins to sweep hard like she's mad at the trash. Mother and my grandmother say she's crazy clean. I'm not so sure she's crazy, but she does clean a lot—more than anybody I've ever seen.

"Hi, Miz Beene," I say as I turn into our walkway. She's so busy sweeping, she sweeps right over my shoes, but she doesn't say anything.

That's why people say Mrs. Beene is strange. She doesn't talk very much. I guess in a whole day, if you counted them, she might say five or six sentences. She just polishes and cleans and mops and sweeps a lot. That's it.

I can feel it when she is going to be friendly, though,
and she really is speaking inside, and I can feel it when she doesn't want to be bothered with me, and if she did talk out loud a lot like everybody else, she probably wouldn't answer back.

Mrs. Beene is tall and skinny and she doesn't look very friendly. When she stares down at you, her eyebrows come together in a V. Her eyes look like two little tiny flashlights shining out of her face, and she keeps her lips pressed together tight like she locked up her mouth and threw away the key.

I was five when we first moved to 6210 Culpepper Street three years ago. Every time I saw her I would cut and run. After a while I got used to the way she looked, and when I found out she had thirteen cats, it seemed too good to be true. We've been friends ever since. I love cats!

She's got all kinds: black ones, gray ones, striped ones, tomcats, black-and-white ones, fluffy ones, fat ones, and skinny ones. They all live in the back storeroom behind the stairs, and they come running out to say hello whenever anybody opens the front door and comes in.

"Radio say this morning it's going to snow tonight," I tell her. "Maybe we should put the flag inside."

Mrs. Beene gives one big swoosh to the trash, and it scatters in the gutter, and she sweeps so hard, the feather on her hat is jiggling up and down. She wears that hat all the time. It's round like a tam, and it is rusty green with a big gray speckled feather on it.

Once I asked her what kind of a feather it was and she said, "Guinea hen."

I'm getting cold standing outside. My toes feel like ten little ice balls, and I bet if I stamped my feet, they'd just break off and roll down the walkway.

"Can I come down and play with the cats this evening, Miz Beene?"

I know she's going to say something, so I jump up and down to keep warm and wait for it to come out. Sometimes I imagine she makes the words way down in her stomach and she has to wait till they float up a long pipe into her mouth.

"Guess so," she says. That's all. But she really means something like this: "Sure, honey, you can come down and play with the cats if you want to."

"Thanks, Miz Beene," I say back. She doesn't look up. She's looking around the yard, seeing if she missed any dirt.

I smell supper cooking as soon as I walk in the door. The cats come to say hello, and they go back into their room. We live on the second floor, and I go up real slow, my feet are so cold. Supper smells like butter beans and bacon. I'm so hungry, I hope my grandmother has the corn bread and milk waiting for me on the table. And that makes me think about the cream puffs and Yoki. I just don't understand why these things happen to me.

I put my books down on a little table in the second-floor hallway just before you get to our door. I am just about to knock when I hear a little "Meow, meow."

Now, where is that coming from? I look around for the kitten making that little sound and I see one of Mrs. Beene's kittens, Spaghetti Sauce, sitting on top of the Victrola. That record player's so old, it's got a big horn on top of it where the sound comes out.

I pick up Spaghetti Sauce and hold her up on my shoulder and rub her back. It feels like silk. Nobody knows that her name is Spaghetti Sauce but me. I named her that because she is the color—orange and white—of spaghetti and tomato sauce.

"Hi, sweet kitty," I say to her. "What you doing up here? You be careful my grandmother don't see you. I don't know why, but she hates cats. Just hates them."

Sauce rubs her soft face up under my chin. I can feel her motor going. If I close my eyes and hardly breathe, it feels like I've got a motor too.

Just then my grandmother opens the door. "Oh!" she screams. "Get that cat outta here!"

Sauce slips right out of my hands, and she's so scared, she runs past my grandmother's feet into our kitchen, and that's the wrong place to be.

"You old, nasty cat, come outta there!" says Grandmother, running after Sauce, who leaps on the stove and knocks over the teakettle. Then she knocks over a cup of soap flakes on the sink shelf. She jumps from there to the icebox, and down comes the potato plant my mother is growing. My grandmother catches her by the leg. She picks her up, holding her straight out in front of her by the back of the neck like she smells bad.

"Don't carry her like that. It hurts!" I say, trying to take Sauce, who has got all her claws stuck out and is making a terrible hard sound in her throat.

"Get outta my way, girl. I'm making sure this troublemaking cat don't never come up here anymore!"

I can't do a thing for Sauce, and she is probably thinking that if she could turn into a tiger or a lion, she would show my grandmother what mean is. But she doesn't turn into anything. Just stays a little tiny kitten being dangled out in space by the skin on her neck.

My grandmother stops at the top of the stairs and then throws the kitten down every one of those steps to the first floor. Sauce gives a cry going down that sounds like she's scared to death.

"That'll teach it a lesson it'll never forget," says my grandmother, breathing hard. She reaches into her apron pocket and pulls out a cigarette and a match. She pops the match on her thumb and lights the cigarette. I don't care if she's got to live with us until the war is over, I'm not saying another word to her. She's done the worst thing I've seen anybody do.

"They ain't no good, them cats," says my grandmother. "Don't know why you so crazy about them, thinking they human beings or somethin'. You and that ole crazy landlady, you make some pair."

"Sauce is not nasty and Mrs. Beene is not crazy!" I say, and then I get scared because I never raise my voice to a grown-up. It's just not done.

"You there, missy, you watch your mouth or you get a swat on your backside. Since you been up here in the

city, you forgettin' your country ways and your country
manners."

I want to say that there is something worse than bad manners and that's a hard heart. But I don't. I just turn away and run down the stairs to see about Sauce.

When I get to the bottom of the stairs, there is no blood, no broken bones, and no Sauce.

"Sauce, where are you?"

I hear my grandmother go inside the kitchen and slam the door. I find Sauce in the storeroom behind the stairs, sitting in the corner with her tail curled around her. She doesn't look hurt at all, just look like her feelings hurt. If it's true that cats have nine lives, this poor cat only got eight left and just got started in life.

I reach out my hand to her, but she snaps out her paw and scratches me.

"It didn't hurt, Sauce, just a little scratch. I know you didn't mean it," I say to her.

"Bob, you, missy, you go on upstairs now and get those school clothes off and into your play things," my grandmother, Sweetmama, says as she comes down the stairs with her coat on. "I got to run down to Yoki's. Heard he got chickens in. Course I don't see why we can't keep a few chickens in the yard—never have to buy another one till the war is over."

She goes quick out the door before the cats can come out of the back room and curl around her ankles.

I don't say a thing, just keep my head down until the door closes. Then I turn around and go back into the room with Sauce. Why should I mind somebody who is so mean? What she did was wrong. Now I wish she never had come to stay with us after my father went into the navy. I wish my mother wasn't working. I guess I wish everything was like it used to be before anybody ever heard of World War II.

I try to sit near Sauce, but she runs down the hall and climbs up on a four-legged table that's round on one side and straight on the side next to the wall. Mrs. Beene keeps it waxed and polished, and there is a little lace cloth on it and on top of that a cut-glass jar. She thinks it makes the hallway look nice. No matter what she does, though, this just a run-down old rooming house.

I try to get Sauce off the table, but she won't move. "Come on, kitty, kitty, I won't hurt you," I say.

I pick her up and up comes the tablecloth, too, because she is holding on to it with her claws. Down crashes the glass jar.

Mrs. Beene hears the noise and comes out of her door. She looks down at me holding Sauce, who has the cloth dangling from her claws.

"I'm sorry, Mrs. Beene," I say. "I didn't know Sauce was holding on to the tablecloth when I picked her up."

Mrs. Beene turns around without a word and goes back inside and comes out again, holding a broom and a dustpan. She starts to sweep up the glass.

I just start to cry and put Sauce down, and she runs back into the storeroom. Mrs. Beene finishes sweeping up the glass, and then she puts the tablecloth back on the table. She stands there holding the glass in the dust-

pan, looking down at me crying. "My . . . my . . .
grandmother threw Sauce down the stairs, Mrs. Beene.
It was awful. . . . I was. . . ."

And then I stop talking. I can't talk about my
grandmother behind her back. I just can't talk against
my own flesh and blood even though she is wrong. In
our family that's the worst thing you can do. So I just
stand there wiping my eyes. Mrs. Beene looks down,
and I guess she sees a tiny piece of glass nobody else
could see, and she sweeps, sweeps again.

When she finishes, she puts down the dustpan and
comes over and pats me on the back. She looks just as
mean as ever because of the V frown between her eyes,
but I know she feels bad for me. She just can't say it.

Mrs. Beene goes back into her rooms, and I walk up
the stairs very slowly.

We live in two rooms. First is the kitchen after you
come in from the hall, and then three steps up is Mother's and my father's bedroom, which everybody calls
the other room. My grandmother and I sleep on a roll-away bed in the kitchen. I used to sleep by myself, but
now my grandmother's snoring wakes me and it seems
like I spend all night long shaking the bed to stop the
noise.

The kitchen is the room where everybody does all
the living and working and playing. I drag my feet real
slow across the kitchen linoleum—it's got teacups
painted all over it—and then I go up the three steps
into the other room. I feel so low, I can't take my
school clothes off.

I don't care what Mrs. Jenkins says, this war better be over soon. Mother says I can't write my father anything to make him worry. But nobody has good news to tell all the time.

I get out the blue, real thin writing paper my father sent me and I sit down at my mother's vanity table and try to write him a letter. I think and I think. I go to the window to see if it's started snowing like my grandmother said it would, but nothing is happening so far. I can't write about that. This is what I finally write:

Dear Daddy,

I know I'm not supposed to write you bad news. Just good news. But today there just isn't anything good to write about. I remember you used to say that when you were a boy, trouble just seemed to follow you around. Well, that's what's happening to me. I don't know why. It just happens.

So I thought I would write you about things we used to do together so you would remember me better, you've been gone so long. Remember when you were teaching me to catch a fish and when I got a bite, you got so excited you backed off the pier and we had to go swimming instead of fishing? I remember that all the time. Sweetmama can jump rope all right but not the way you can. I've been practicing these double skips like you showed me, and maybe if I ever meet Joe Louis I'll show him how he don't have a thing on me because I can do boxer jump rope too.

Remember when Shirley saw you jumping and her mouth flew open, she was so surprised? She is still

my best friend like I hope you and her daddy Leon
are. Do you ever see him? I know he's in the army
and you're in the navy, but I thought maybe by
accident you saw him walking on the street. It sure
would be a good thing if you could play cards together
over there like you used to do here.

I guess that's all I want to write for now.

I love you (smile) *Bob*

I put the letter in my arithmetic book to mail tomorrow. And then I lay across my mother's bed and wish
she would come home. This day has been terrible. Yoki
might get sick, he ate our dessert; I can't ever talk to
my grandmother because of what she did; and then
Sauce and I broke Mrs. Beene's jar.

I can't believe all of this happened to me in just one
hour or so after school.

3

WORLD WAR II

:24   Sweetmama comes back in from the store. "What you doing laying across the bed with your good clothes still on?" she asks.

I don't answer. I just turn my head away. How could she do that to Sauce? She's supposed to be my grandmother. She's supposed to want me to be happy, not sad like this.

"All right, you lay there if you want, missy, but your mother be home soon. She'll deal with you."

When she goes back into the kitchen, I close my eyes, I'm so tired, and the next thing I know I'm waking up

and the room is dark and there is a quilt over me. I
guess my grandmother put it there, but that don't cut
no ice with me.

I can hear her moving around in the kitchen, getting
the table set for supper. Then I hear her strike a match
to light her cigarette and the air whistling out of the
chair cushion when she sits down at the table. Gabriel
Heatter is talking in his scary voice on the news. He
always makes it sound like we're in big trouble, and
chill bumps come up on my arms when he starts talking
about the American soldiers killed in the Pacific and
the European theaters. I'm always afraid he is going to
say the name John Henry Weathers. But Mother keeps
telling me he'll never do that. "What makes you think
of all the thousands of men fighting in the war, he's
going to up and call out your father's name?" she asked
me. " 'Cause he's my father," I want to say.

I close my eyes in the dark and try to remember my
daddy's face. I wonder what he's doing right now.
Wouldn't it be funny if he was wondering what I was
doing right now?

I couldn't eat for a week when he left. He told me he
had to go because of Pearl Harbor and the Japanese
bombing it.

I don't know how far Pearl Harbor in Hawaii is ex-
actly from St. Louis, where we live, but it must be very
close, because when the enemy bombed Pearl Harbor,
everybody on the radio was talking very scared like any
minute the planes going to come flying over and bomb
our city too.

That night Mother, Daddy, and me sat around the radio listening. One radio announcer said, "Everybody will long remember December 7, 1941." I was sitting on my daddy's lap, and he kept hugging me to his chest.

The next day President Roosevelt said we were at war. "The whole world fighting each other," my daddy said. "I guess I got to go."

I wrapped my arms tight around his neck and shut my eyes. I wished I could close up my ears too. I didn't want to hear him say he was going to go off where people being shot, being blowed up and never seen again.

Daddy kept saying he knew how I felt, but that didn't stop him from sitting down and writing my grandmother down South and asking her to come and live with Mother and me until he got back.

I didn't want anybody to come and stay with me. But after Mother said she would go work for the "war effort," making things to help the soldiers fight, Daddy said he didn't want me coming home to an empty house.

I hear Mother's key in the door. She says hello to Sweetmama and then she says, "Where's Bob?"

"She's in the other room pouting," says Sweetmama.

"How come she doing that?" asks Mother.

"She mad, acting like she all hurt because I threw one of the crazy landlady's cats off this floor."

"No wonder she feels bad," says Mother. "You know Bob can't stand to see nothin' hurt."

"You know good and well throwing no cat down twelve little steps ain't going to hurt it," says Sweet-

mama. Now she sounds like she's getting mad. I hope
she gets so mad, she packs up and goes back home.

"Ain't no need you getting so hot about it," says
Mother.

"Look here, Saree," says Grandmother, "I ain't
going to sit here and talk no more about no nasty cat.
They just sets my teeth on edge. If I'd a known all those
cats squirmin' round this place, I woulda never come."

I sure wish she had known.

My mother comes into the room and snaps on the
light at her vanity table. "Bob," she says, "whatchoo
doing laying down in the dark like that?"

"She hurt Sauce!" I say.

"That must have hurt your feelings bad," Mother
says, coming over and putting her arms around me.
"But we going to talk about this when we by ourselves,
not now, you hear?"

"But . . ."

Mother shakes her head and puts her finger up to her
lips. Then she whispers, "Your grandmother a guest in
this house. It's not polite to talk about her, she's sitting
right in the next room."

"But I need to tell you . . ."

"Bob," she says, raising her eyebrows, "that's
enough. Now, come on in the kitchen. Time for supper."

I can't believe she's just worrying about my grandmother's feelings and not mine, but all I say is, "Yes,
ma'am."

I put on my nightgown and I go into the kitchen
holding on to Rose. She's a stuffed rabbit been with me

since I was a baby. She used to be pink, but she's gray now. I sit Rose in the chair with me and I don't look up from my plate.

"When you going to grow outta that rabbit?" asks my grandmother.

I don't answer. I just keep my head down.

Sweetmama and Mother talk, but when they say something to me, I just say "Yes, ma'am" and "No, ma'am" and that's it.

"Ooh, wee," says Mother, "this is worse than World War Two right here at this table."

After supper Mother starts to pull out the roll-away bed. "Bob, you go out to the bathroom and wash your face and brush your teeth," she says. "Hurry up too, before that Mrs. Walker from upstairs gets in. You know she stay in there so long, you think she planting corn waiting for it to grow."

One bad thing about a rooming house is you only rent rooms. You don't have a bathroom of your own. We're lucky because the bathroom is next door to our rooms, but we have to share it with Mrs. Walker and Mrs. Walker's mother, who is sick and who plays the radio morning, noon, and night. If Mrs. Walker leaves her rooms to go to work or to the store, her mother starts to call, "Lucille, Lucille, where you?"

Mrs. Beene takes care of her when Mrs. Walker goes to work, but no matter what, Mrs. Walker's mother still calls for her until she gets home.

The bathroom door is closed. Mrs. Walker beat me to it. I sit down to wait outside in front of the door.

I wish I had brought Rose out to keep me company, I wait so long. Then I begin to think that maybe Mrs. Walker took a bath and drowned in the bathtub. The more I wait, the more I think that's just what happened in there. Drowned.

I put my ear flat to the door, but I can't hear anything. Suppose she is drowned for real? I tap on the door. No answer. I tap again, harder, and I jump when Mrs. Walker says in a loud voice, "Yes, whose botherin' that door?"

"Just me, Mrs. Walker."

"Oh, Barbara, I'll be out in a minute."

Mrs. Walker comes out from the bathroom carrying some magazines under her arm. "Onliest time I get some peace and a chance to read," she says as she passes by and pats me on the head. I bet she's been sitting in that big old armchair in front of the window reading while I wait outside. Suppose I really had to go bad. That wouldn't cut no ice with her.

The bathroom is a big room, and Mrs. Beene tries to make it nice, since everybody on the second and third floor got to use it. She put in the big chair, and there is a footstool too. The chair got some springs poking from under the bottom, but other than that it feels good to sit in. I curl up in it after I brush my teeth. I call this my thinking chair. When there's something bothering me, I come in here and close the door and just sit in this chair and think about it. Mrs. Walker is right, this is the only place to come for some peace and quiet. But before I can think about Yoki or what I'm going to do about Sweetmama, Mother knocks at the door.

"Bob, don't stay all night. Bedtime."

After I say my prayers, I get into bed and put my arm across my eyes to keep out the light. Sweetmama is sitting at the kitchen table doing her embroidery. I look at her through a little space under my arm. She doesn't look so bad. She looks like she used to before she was so cruel to Sauce.

She's holding her embroidery in one hand and poking the needle with some pink thread in it into the cloth. Then she sets down the round hoop holding the embroidery and picks up her cigarette. She takes a smoke and shakes off the ash and puts it back between her lips, and she squints through the smoke at her embroidery. She says smoking is a bad habit, but she still smokes one cigarette after another all day long. She says she just can't help it.

I turn over and pull the cover up over my ears. I try to keep my eyes open so I can think about things, but it's hard. When I close them, I see a girl standing on a tall mountain that comes to a point at the top like a pyramid. There are steps cut on the side all the way down; maybe a thousand. She steps off the point and begins to fall out in space very slowly, with her arms and legs splayed out like spokes on a wheel, and she turns around and around and floats like a snowflake.

The next thing I know it's morning, and Mother is leaning over me.

"The day passin' you by, Bob," she says, kissing me. She hands me a fresh towel and a bar of soap and clean clothes. And I start for the bathroom.

"You forgot something, Bob?" asks Mother.

"No, ma'am," I say.

"You didn't say good morning to your grand-mother."

I keep my eyes down. "Morning."

"Well, that ain't much," says Sweetmama.

I run quickly out of the kitchen and close the door. I wash up fast and put my clothes on. Today is Saturday, and it's a good day because Mother and I spend time together without Sweetmama. She's too busy going to the rummage sale and over to the church to roll bandages for the war and to prayer meeting.

"What we going to do today?" I ask Mother when we're washing the breakfast dishes.

"Maybe a movie later," she says. "Got to go to Yoki's Grocery Store now," she says, going into the other room to get her coat and hat. "Saw old man Strausburger delivering the milk this morning, and he says he's going to have sugar and butter in today. I've been waiting for that. Got to put the sugar away for our Easter cake. Not but a couple of months away."

"You saw Yoki pulling the wagon?" I ask. That means that he didn't get sick from those cream puffs, I think to myself.

"He was pulling it like he always do."

"Did he look all right?"

"If you ask me, he ain't never looked all right. He's one mangy old horse. Looks like the moths got at him on a rainy day," she says and laughs as she stoops down and pulls her pocketbook from behind the skirt under the sink. "Old man Strausburger look sick to me. Coughing so much, I think he's going to throw up."

I start to turn circles in the kitchen, I'm so happy Yoki isn't sick.

"How come you want to know if Yoki is all right?" she asks.

"I just do, that's all."

Then she looks down at me the way she does when she is going to read my mind.

"Whatchoo up to? You got in some trouble again?"

I don't say anything. I'm not supposed to lie, so I try not to say a thing.

"Bob?"

Before I have to tell her, the downstairs doorbell rings two shorts and a long. That's our ring.

"Probably the iceman. I put the sign in the window for twenty-five pounds," says Mother.

I run down and let Henry the iceman in. He's the widest person I know, and he isn't fat, just strong, because he carries big blocks of ice on his shoulder so people with iceboxes can keep their food cold. He starts up the stairs all bent over, carrying the ice with a metal clamp that looks like big scissors with sharp points on the end that stick into the ice and hold it.

I run quick and open the top of the icebox so Henry can slip the ice in.

He gives a big "oomph," leans his shoulder in, and that big, square chunk of ice slides right in.

"When this war is over," says Mother after Henry

leaves, "there are going to be some changes made. I'm getting me a refrigerator. No more putting the card in the window show how much ice we need. No more iceman."

Mother is always saying that changes are going to be made after the war about anything she doesn't like.

"Now, you be good," says Mother, putting on her coat. "I'll probably be an hour, if that line ain't around the block already. When this war is over, there's one thing I ain't never going to do again and that's stand in line. Only one line I'm going to stand in and that's to get into the Pearly Gates," she says, laughing and going out the door. My mother can be funny sometimes.

After I hear her going down the stairs, I start to sing, "Yoki's all right, Yoki's all right, yeah, yeah, yeah."

I feel like dancing with somebody, I'm so happy. But nobody's here but me and the sink and the stove, the table, the roll-away bed, and the icebox. The sink's got a blue skirt around it got flowers and writing all over it that say, In France we say "Oui, Oui." My grandmother found it at a church rummage. The stove is metal, got feet like paws on it, but it can't dance. When I was little, I used to believe that after everybody went to sleep, the stove would tiptoe out the door on those paws and meet the bathtub who's got paws too, and they would clank down the stairs and go play in the backyard. Maybe I saw that in a dream.

But that stove can't do a thing but sit there, so I just whirl around and around until the stove, the sink, everything, starts spinning around right before my eyes.

4

A TERRIBLE DISCOVERY

Every Saturday Mrs. Beene gets down on her hands and knees and scrubs and waxes the hallways. And then she puts newspapers down on the floors so nobody can mess them up. The next week she takes up the newspapers and cleans the floors all over again and puts more newspapers down. The halls never get a chance to get dirty.

She has just finished putting all the newspapers down again when Chuckie and his mother, Mrs. Williams, come to visit. I start to squinch up my eyes and get

mad. I've been so busy, I forgot all about planning
what I was going to do to get Chuckie. What I hate the
most is, my mother and his mother are best friends, and
they visit us a lot or we visit them down on the end of
the block on Culpepper Street, and usually Chuckie
does something to make me mad.

When Mrs. Beene opens the door for them, I am
downstairs in the back room playing with the cats. Mrs.
Williams just nods at Mrs. Beene. I heard her tell
Mother that she thinks Mrs. Beene is "touched in the
head."

I poke my head around the door of the back room
and say, "Hi, Mrs. Williams." I pretend Chuckie's not
even there.

"Hi you, sugar," says Mrs. Williams. "Your mama
upstairs?"

She goes upstairs, and Chuckie follows her but turns
around on the stairs to give me a nasty look and to grin
at Mrs. Beene, who is giving him a mean look for real.
I guess she feels about Chuckie the way I do. Probably
worse, because one time Chuckie tied her doorknob to
the stair post and she couldn't get out of her room.

I stay downstairs helping Mrs. Beene. Mother calls
down, "Bob, girl, you down there, come up. You got
company."

Company. Chuckie's not company. My girl friends
Shirley and Audrey are company, because I want them
to visit, but I don't think somebody who comes over
because his mother says he has to and that I don't want
to play with is my company.

"Mrs. Beene just took in the flag," I announce when I get upstairs. Chuckie's busy putting old records on the Victrola in the hallway. Mother and Mrs. Williams are sitting around the table in the kitchen with the door to the kitchen propped open.

"Saw a few snowflakes coming down," Mrs. Williams says.

"That so?" says Mother, getting up. "Better go get those clothes off the line. Don't want them to get wet after it take so long for them to dry in this cold."

She and Mrs. Williams go downstairs, and Chuckie leaves the record going around and around and runs down the stairs after them. I go to the side window and look down on them. The snowflakes start to come down thicker right before my eyes. At first there are just a few blowing in the wind, and then they start whirling in circles and more and more of them start coming down. Mother and Mrs. Williams work fast. The clothes so stiff, they look like they've got starch in them because the water has frozen in them. Mother drops a pair of my snuggins, and Chuckie quick picks them up and starts balancing them on his head. Oooh, I'm so embarrassed. I don't like to wear long underwear come down to my knees like those snuggins, but I have to when it's cold, and nobody but my mother and my grandmother has ever seen them. Now Chuckie knows about them. If he comes upstairs and says a thing to me about them, I'm leaving. I'm going down to Mrs. Beene's and keep her company.

I don't get a chance to tell Chuckie what I think of

him because Mother tells us to take two paper bags full of tin cans she's been saving and flatten them out and then take them down to Yoki's Grocery Store. "There's a tin drive on for the war, and I been saving these for a month."

While Chuckie gets his boots, coat, and hat on, I go into the other room and put on a pair of pants under my skirt. "Bob, be sure to put a sweater on under that coat," says Mother.

We take the bags down into the yard and have a good time stamping on the cans and mashing them flat. I forget all about how terrible Chuckie is and how mad I am at him. He's being so nice to me and he can be fun if he wants to. That's how he is.

When we finish, we can't tell one can from another. The store won't take them unless they are flat and the labels are off so you can't tell the cut-corn from the string-bean cans.

We start off to the store. "Chuckie, come on," I say. "I want to get to Yoki's store in a hurry so I have time to visit with Yoki for a while."

"Mr. Strausburger let you play with Yoki?" Chuckie asks, looking at me like he just started thinking I'm a pretty good person.

"Yep," I say, proud I have been doing something he never thought of.

"I don't believe it."

"You'll see."

"Well, come on then," he says. "Why you walking so slow!"

Inside, the store is not busy like yesterday. And Mr. Strausburger is not there. Some other man, who looks like Mr. Strausburger only he's younger and doesn't have a bald head, is standing behind the counter.

"Mr. Strausburger here?"

"Not today. Not for a lot of days," says the man, smiling and showing a big space between his two front teeth.

I don't care if he is smiling. I don't like him very much. That's another thing about me. I know right away whether I'm going to like a person I first meet. I don't have to get to know him.

"Where is he?" I ask.

"He's sick. I'm his nephew, Roger. And who are you two?" he asks, still smiling.

"I'm Barbara, and this is Chuckie."

"Charles," says Chuckie.

"Well, Barbara and Charles, what do you have there? More tin cans to make tin tanks?" he says, and he laughs. "Heh, heh, heh," not like Mr. Strausburger at all.

"Who's going to drive the milk wagon?" I ask, taking the tin cans to the back storeroom.

Before I can go behind the counter, Roger says, "Wait a minute. Who told you you could go behind the counter?"

"I always do," I say, standing with my lower lip poked out and my hands on my hips. When I do that, watch out, I'm ready to fight.

"Well, my uncle is upstairs very sick, and now I'm in

charge here," he says. "No going behind the counter
unless you have my permission."

I stand there staring at him with my eyes all
squinched up.

"Well, all right, you can go back and put those cans
in with the others," he says, laughing like he thinks
I'm funny.

"Come on, Chuckie," I say.

"I don't like him," I whisper to Chuckie when we are
in the back room.

Chuckie is not listening. He's too busy looking at the
stacks of tin cans going all the way up to the ceiling.

"There must be a thousand here. I wonder what they
do with them when we send them off to be used for the
war."

"Maybe that'll tell you," I say, pointing to a big sign
on the door of the storeroom.

It said: One old lawn mower will help make six
bullets and one old tire will help make twelve gas
masks and an old shovel will help make four hand
grenades. It didn't say what tin cans would make.

When we finish stacking our cans, we go back into
the store and I ask Roger again, "Who's going to deliver the milk?"

"You want the job?" asks Roger, laughing again.

"You know you wouldn't give me the job," I say,
disgusted.

"If you must know, Henry the iceman is going to be
the new milkman from now on before he starts his ice
deliveries. He's got a good wagon and a strong horse;

there's no reason he can't take over."

"What about Yoki?" I ask.

"Yoki, I'm sad to say, will be sold on Monday to the glue factory."

"You kiddin' me," I say, my voice shaking.

"Might be; might not," says Roger, laughing.

"Mr. Strausburger wouldn't let you."

"Oh, I don't know about that. My uncle is retiring. He'll be turning everything over to me."

I look closer at Roger, trying to tell whether he is kidding or telling the truth. The only thing I can tell for sure is that I don't like him a bit.

"But Mr. Strausburger loves Yoki," I say. "He would never let you sell him to make . . . to make . . ."

"Glue," says Chuckie. I look around at him ready to fight, but he doesn't look like he's teasing me. He looks like I feel—mad at Roger—and he doesn't even know Yoki. That's what I mean. When Chuckie is good, he's the best.

"Well, anything else I can do for you two?" asks Roger, starting to put some cans on the shelves.

"We would like to visit with Yoki."

"Help yourself," says Roger. "That old horse needs somebody to talk with him. Soon's I can, I'll be putting him out of his misery. He's going to rest in peace."

Chuckie and I go into the back through the storeroom and out into the yard.

"What does that mean, 'Rest in peace'?" I ask Chuckie.

"They say that when somebody dies. You know, at

the funeral they say, 'Rest in peace.' "

"You think he's kidding?"

"Maybe. I don't know. If he is telling the truth, I just don't think it's right to do that to a horse or anybody," says Chuckie, and I just love him for saying that.

"I don't believe it," I say. "I don't believe Mr. Strausburger will let Roger sell Yoki. Yoki's like his family. He told me he's had him for fifteen years."

We open the shed door and go inside. Yoki looks good, not like he ate a slice of sweet-potato pie, three cream puffs, and some wax paper yesterday. "Hi you, Yoki," I say, untying him from the post.

"How come you do that? Going to let him out?" asks Chuckie, his eyes lighting up. He always starts to get happy when he thinks he's going to do something he's not supposed to do.

"I always do it. He's not going anywhere," I say.

"Yoki, this is Chuckie," I say. "You've seen him lots of times."

"You talking to that horse like he can understand you," says Chuckie.

"Who's to say he doesn't?" I say.

"Hi, Yoki," says Chuckie. "Can I get up on your back?"

"I don't think he'll like that. He's never carried anybody. He just pulls the milk wagon."

But as usual he doesn't listen. He shinnies up the post next to Yoki and then throws his arms over Yoki's back and pulls himself up. "I'm Tonto, and this is my horse, Scout."

Yoki just stretches his front legs out in front of him and puts his head down and makes a sliding board out of his neck and shoulders. Chuckie slides right off with his legs straight up in the air and lands on the ground.

"Ow!" he says.

I can't do a thing but laugh and laugh.

Yoki's just standing there, and he looks like he's smiling too.

After we finish visiting with Yoki, Chuckie and I go back through the storeroom and are just about to come into the store when we hear Roger talking on the telephone to somebody.

"How are you feeling, Uncle Ben?" he says. He must be talking with Mr. Strausburger upstairs.

"You just take it easy. I've arranged with the iceman to take over the milk route. Yes, that's right. Okay. I've been telling you for a long time that running this store and delivering the milk was too much. No . . . Yoki? . . . Don't worry about him. A man is coming on Monday to buy him. . . . Yes, I know, Uncle, but he's an old horse. He needs to be put out of his misery."

When we hear this, we look at each other, scared. "He wasn't kidding," I say to Chuckie.

"I know," says Chuckie, looking worried.

"He can't do that," I say, but Chuckie puts his finger up to his lips. "Shhhh," he whispers. "Let's pretend we didn't hear him."

"Whatchoo mean?" I say, but he gives me a dirty look, and I shut up. I don't know what else to say, anyway.

We come out from the back and start for the door. "You kids have a nice visit with Yoki?" asks Roger.

"Sure did," says Chuckie as if we never heard a thing.

"That's good," he says, smiling.

Chuckie is holding my hand very tight so that I won't say anything.

"You kids welcome to come back tomorrow and see the poor old horse. The store is closed on Sunday, but the side gate is never locked, and you can go on in so long as you close the gate when you leave."

"We sure will," says Chuckie, very polite. And then he drags me out of there.

When we get outside, the snow is coming down thick.

"Chuckie," I say, "maybe we can go to the police, have Mr. Strausburger's nephew arrested for sending Yoki off to be killed."

"Ain't no law against it. Police would just laugh at you."

"You mean if somebody just came up and shot a dog, just for nothing, they wouldn't be put in jail?"

"Where you been? I knew that when I was eight."

"Well, you don't know everything!" I say, picking up some snow and throwing it at him. I'm so worried about Yoki and so mad, I feel like throwing snow at everybody. I feel like kicking somebody.

"Maybe we could rescue him," says Chuckie.

"How we going to do that?"

"I don't know," says Chuckie, "but we got to do something."

5

CHUCKIE MAKES A FRIEND

:44 On the way home we don't say much. We're trying to think. I don't want to make Chuckie feel bad, but I can't help thinking that there is nothing a ten-year-old and a person who is almost nine years old can do to save a horse.

"You know something, Chuckie, this is the worst winter I've ever had. First my father's been away almost a year in the war and then my grandmother hates cats and now Yoki is going to be killed. It's too much!"

As we come up to the walkway of the rooming house, we see Mrs. Beene out front shoveling the snow off the walk.

"How come she's shoveling the snow?" Chuckie
asks. "It's still coming down."

"She just feels like it, I guess," I say.

"That's the first time I ever seen anybody do that," says Chuckie.

"Hey," I say, "you just better worry about keeping out of trouble with Mrs. Beene. She can put you in a dark room in her house with a stuffed dog she keeps."

"You kiddin' me."

I just shrug.

"She ever say anything?"

"All the time."

"I never heard her."

"She doesn't talk to people that do bad things to her like you did," I say.

Mrs. Beene is starting back up the steps into the house when we catch up with her.

"Hi, Miz Beene," I say. She puts the broom over her shoulder but she doesn't say anything.

Chuckie pokes me in the ribs with his elbow, and it hurts even through my coat and sweaters.

"Ouch, Chuckie!"

Mrs. Beene turns around and gives him her worst look. "Leave her alone," she says to Chuckie, who looks surprised. He really must have believed that Mrs. Beene couldn't talk.

"That's all right, Mrs. Beene," I say. "Chuckie and me, we're friends now, and we got one big problem."

She looks down at me as if to say, "You ain't kiddin' me, are you?"

"No, really, Chuckie's changing. He even said he was sorry he tied up your door."

Chuckie cuts his eyes at me, but I pretend I don't see him.

We line up our boots near the front door next to the flag, and Mrs. Beene looks at us like she thinks we are two good kids for doing that.

"Come on," she says.

And we follow her into her rooms. Chuckie stops at the door and looks around.

"I was just kiddin' you, Chuckie, there isn't a stuffed dog in here," I say, laughing.

Chuckie looks like he wants to punch me, but he doesn't. I put my hand up to my mouth to stop from giggling.

We go into the kitchen, and as Mrs. Beene is putting her apron on, she looks at me as if to say, "Now, why he think there is a dog here?"

Mrs. Beene takes our coats and hangs them on a hook. And she takes out a jar of cookies and puts them on the table.

I like Mrs. Beene's kitchen a lot. She's got Christmas cards, Easter cards, cards for when you're sick, all kinds of cards, tacked up all over the walls. She's even got them on the ceiling so that you can hardly see any wall in her kitchen. There are so many colors that I feel like I'm inside a box of crayons. She's also got little flower stick-ons on the stove doors and the icebox and the kitchen-cabinet doors. They're on the cups and

saucers, the cookie jar, and just about anything you can
stick them on.

"Ummm," says Chuckie, crunching down on one of
Mrs. Beene's cookies. I can see he's beginning to like
Mrs. Beene better already. I feel good myself, but then
I don't. I remember what's going to happen to Yoki on
Monday.

When Mrs. Beene sits down after giving us cups of
lemon tea with a slice of onion in it, I tell her. "Something terrible's going to happen to Yoki. Mr. Strausburger is sick, and his nephew wants to stop delivering
the milk and have the iceman do it, and the iceman
already has a horse and wagon, so Roger says he's
going to sell Yoki to the glue-factory people."

Mrs. Beene looks as if to say, "Are you sure that's
what's happening?"

"We overheard him telling Mr. Strausburger it's
going to happen on Monday," says Chuckie.

Mrs. Beene shakes her head from side to side like
she's saying, "Ain't that a shame."

"Where's the horse?" she asks. And Chuckie jumps a
little. He didn't expect her to say anything. That's
what's interesting about Mrs. Beene. You never know
when she's going to talk out loud.

"He's behind the store," says Chuckie.

"It's not fair that Yoki is going to be killed for glue,"
I say. "Every time I turn around, somebody being
killed. They're killing people in the war and that's all
you hear on the radio, and now they're killing Yoki for

no reason except they don't want him anymore. Why can't they give him to somebody else?"

"Maybe it's too much trouble, don't want to be bothered finding somebody to give him to," says Chuckie.

Mrs. Beene just looks so sad, like she's going to cry.

"Maybe we can rescue Yoki," Chuckie says. "My boy-scout leader says it's our duty to help others. I don't know whether he meant a horse."

Mrs. Beene's flashlight eyes seem to cut right into us. She looks excited, like Chuckie does when he thinks we are going to do something we're not supposed to do.

There is a knock at the door, and Mrs. Beene goes to answer it. My mother says, "Mrs. Beene, these children driving you crazy?" She looks embarrassed. I know she's thinking that Mrs. Beene maybe is a little crazy.

Mrs. Beene goes to get our coats and hands them to Mother without saying a word.

"I'm sorry if they have," says Mother, talking extra nice, "but now it's time for them to come up for their supper."

"Thanks for the cookies, Mrs. Beene," I say as we go up the stairs.

"Me too," says Chuckie.

Mrs. Beene winks at us and then goes back into her rooms.

Mother tells us to go right into the bathroom and wash our hands. While we are in there Chuckie says, "I like Mrs. Beene. Now I'm kinda sorry I tied her door so she couldn't get out, but it was funny."

"We better think of something to do about Yoki or

it's not going to be funny to go to the ten-cent store and
look at those bottles of glue and think he's inside," I
say.

I think hard.

"Maybe we could hide him somewhere," I say.

"But where? Who will take care of him?"

"I bet if we think about it, we know a lot of good
hiding places. That's all we did last summer was find
hideouts, remember."

"Yeah, but most of the time you and Shirley and
Audrey were doing the hiding from me."

"That won't happen anymore, Chuckie," I say. "From
now on we going to be friends."

"Well, maybe," he says.

"Bob and Chuckie," Mother calls, "come on out of
there; your supper's getting cold."

Chuckie and I are quiet at supper.

"What you two doing at Mrs. Beene's?" asks Mother.

"She asked us to come in and have some cookies and
lemon tea with her," says Chuckie.

"She really say that?" asks Mother. "She said to you,
'Come on in have some cookies'?"

"Well . . . she didn't say it, but . . ."

"You mean you invite yourself in without being
asked?"

"She wanted us to come. She just didn't say it," says
Chuckie.

"What's wrong with her, anyway?" asks Mrs. Williams.

"I don't think nothin's wrong with her," Mother

says. "She just had a hard life, from what I hear. Used to live on a farm outside a town called Vidalia. Her husband and her brother got killed in a fire on the farm, and she just couldn't stand to stay there so she come to St. Louis and got a job taking care of this old ramshackle place. That's all I know. She don't socialize and she don't go to church. She just stay right here and clean, clean, clean. And her son takes care of the farm."

Mrs. Williams just shakes her head and says, "Umph, umph, umph, the stories people have to tell. You just never know."

"Now, how come you two so quiet?" asks Mother. "You been fighting again?"

"No, ma'am."

"Well, then, you must be coming down with something. Ever since you been babies together, you been fighting and making up and fighting," Mrs. Williams says and laughs.

We just look at each other. We got something more important to worry about than what our mothers are saying.

Chuckie and I go out in the hallway and put a record on the Victrola.

"If we hid him, where could we do it?" asks Chuckie.

"Shhh," I say and take his hand and lead him up to the top of the third-floor landing. "Why can't we hide him down by the river? Last summer I saw a lot of places to hide where nobody would ever come."

"Yeah, like Mrs. Clay's old shack," says Chuckie.

"That's a good idea, Chuckie," I say. "Nobody'd ever think of going inside a place used to be somebody's house to look for a horse."

"But how are we going to get him there?"

"We are going to have to sneak him, that's all," I say.

"Chuckie, it's time to go home," Mrs. Williams calls out.

"I'll come by tomorrow. Ask your mother if you can help me tie up newspapers for the war drive. They're in our basement," whispers Chuckie just before we get to our hallway.

"Come on, Chuckie, this is Saturday night. Bath time," his mother calls.

"Oh, no," says Chuckie.

"See you tomorrow," I say to Chuckie in a voice that sounds like Gabriel Heatter, and I try to look at him as if to say, "Tomorrow we do something or Yoki is lost."

My mother is taking down the big round washtub from a hook on the wall, and she already has a kettle and two pots of water warming on the stove. I never take a bath in the bathroom tub, because Mother says she doesn't like to be taking a bath in a tub that's not ours.

She sets out the castile soap to wash my hair and the Ivory soap for my bath and the Johnson's Baby Oil to rub on after my bath and then the Cashmere Bouquet powder to shake all over before I put my nightgown on. Baths are not so bad once you get started, but just thinking about taking them makes me tired.

Mother unbraids my hair and combs it until it is like a black cloud all around my head. Then I get into the tub of warm water, and she scrubs my back. Next she washes my hair, and my neck feels like it's going to break off, I have to hold my head down so long.

"You remember yesterday I say we going to talk about your grandmother throwing Sauce down the stairs," Mother says.

I can't say a thing. I'm too busy trying to keep water out of my ears and nose.

"I just want you to forgive your grandmother, Bob," says Mother. "And I want you to know that I think what she did to Sauce was wrong, but everybody can make a mistake. I make mistakes too."

"How come she don't say she's sorry to me?"

"I think she wants to, but she's old-fashioned, brought up to think children supposed to respect grown-ups no matter what the grown-ups do."

"That's not fair," I say as Mother rubs a towel through my hair to get all the water out.

"You right, it ain't," she says. "But lots of things ain't fair. You just got to understand it."

"Well, I don't understand it," I say.

"Now I'm going to tell you a secret."

"What?"

"Your grandmother is afraid of cats."

"She don't act like she's scared of them."

"But she is. That's a fact."

"When you scared of something, you run away from

it. You don't run after it and try to catch it and then :53 throw it down some stairs."

"If she was a little girl, she probably would run away, but she thinks she's got to act different because she's all grown up. So she did the wrong thing. There's something you can do to help her, and I'll be proud of you if you do it."

"What's that?"

"You make sure that the cats are not in the hallway when she comes in if you're at home. If she sees that you trying to make it easier for her, she won't be so hard on those cats."

"Well, I'll try, but I don't know . . ."

"Just try it. I'm not trying to tell you that wrong is right, because it's not. But she's your own flesh and blood, and the good things she do more than the bad. She is a second mother to you, a mother two times over. That's why we call her Sweetmama.

"She's over there at the church rummage all morning looking for nice, quality clothes for you. She do that because she loves you. She ain't perfect, though," Mother says, rubbing some Vaseline into my hair and then starting to comb it out.

"Ouch!" I hate this part. It feels like she's pulling my hair right out of my head.

After Mother finish combing my hair, I climb on her lap and lay my head on her shoulder.

"You promise you try to do better?"

"Yes, ma'am," I say. I'm too tired to talk about it anymore, and I start to worry about Yoki again.

"Yoki is being sold on Monday," I say to Mother as we make some popcorn balls for my grandmother. That's her favorite thing.

"That right?"

"Um-huh, and he's going to be killed for glue."

"That's a shame," says Mother, but she don't act like she really think it's a shame. She's just saying something because I'm saying something. So I don't talk about it anymore. She wouldn't understand.

When Sweetmama comes in, Mother says, "Hi you, Sweetmama, we been waiting up for you."

My grandmother hangs up her coat, and she doesn't seem too happy to see us.

Mother presses my hand and nods at me.

"We made you some popcorn balls," I say so soft, nobody can hear me.

"Speak up, girl," says Sweetmama, frowning. "Whatchoo say?"

I say louder, "I say, we made you some popcorn balls, Sweetmama."

"Now, ain't that nice," my grandmother says, and she comes over and gives me a hug. She hugs me so hard, I can feel the pin she's wearing pressing against my cheek. It's shaped like a drop of blood, and she got it for giving a lot of blood to the Red Cross.

After we eat the popcorn, Mother turns down the roll-away bed and puts on clean sheets and pillowcases. I climb into bed, and they are still sitting around the table talking about what Miss Pearl said and Miss

Audreen and Miss Mary said while Sweetmama was rolling bandages.

"Bob, you don't read too long now, hear? We got Sunday school and church tomorrow."

I am reading *Black Beauty* again because I'm trying to find out how to hitch up a horse to a wagon. Tomorrow Chuckie and I got to do it even though we have never done it before.

It feels good laying on my bed still smelling like soap and bath powder and the kitchen smelling like popcorn and butter and Karo Syrup; and my mother and grandmother to keep me company. I feel so good, I don't think about how much I miss my father. But then I start to think about Yoki standing behind the grocery store right now not knowing that on Monday he is going to be sold to the glue factory.

6

THE SECRET TRIP

:56   The whole world is white!

I've been looking out the window, too excited to leave it and get dressed for church. There is snow covering everything. I've never seen so much snow. It's like nobody ever lived out there before.

"What a sight," says Mother, looking over my shoulder. "Everything covered with ice look like crystal glass—the best you can buy. Snow reminds me of wedding-cake frosting. I mean those big tall cakes you see in the movies. It don't look real, but it's more than real. Ain't nobody but the man above could make that last night."

"Pancakes on the table," Sweetmama says, but I can't leave the window.

"Mother, can I have some snow ice cream after breakfast?"

"Girl, you kiddin' me," says my mother. "Don't seem right to be making snow ice cream this early in the morning. Besides, we got to get ready for church."

"It won't take long," I say. "Remember, Daddy used to go out and get some snow anytime it first came."

"Well, all right. I guess your daddy did tramp out in that snow up to his waist. Dish up some snow before the coal dust settle on it. Back in the country, though, we always wait for second snowfall. First supposed to make the air sweet."

I eat in a hurry and I help Mother on with her galoshes and I get down the biggest bowl we have and a cooking spoon.

"I just hope this snow ain't up to my chin," says Mother, laughing.

I run over to the window to watch her down below, lifting her knees up high and then putting her feet down slowly in the snow. It does come up above her galoshes.

Mother bends and dips, bends and dips until the bowl is piled so high with fluffy white snow that it's as tall as the bowl.

When she comes back upstairs, I quick take the bowl and set it on the table.

"Hope there's no air raid tonight," says Mother, taking out the condensed milk, the sugar, and the vanilla. "Moon be out after such a snow and shining down on all this white, won't matter we got the lights off and the shades down, we be shining bright as day."

"You think that will happen?" I ask, feeling scared in the bottom of my stomach.

"No, honey. I really don't think so. Just a thought, though."

Mother carefully pours Pet milk in the middle of the snow, making a hole all the way down to the bottom, and then she sprinkles lots of sugar on top and next, two teaspoons of vanilla flavoring, and she mixes it together very slowly so that the snow won't spill over the sides. When it starts to look heavy and rich and the color of the Pet milk, then it's ready to eat. I love to hear the crisp sloshing sound the spoon makes dipping in and out of the ice cream.

I get down three bowls and three spoons. "Sweetmama, you having some?" I ask.

"Kinda strange to be eating ice cream 'fore day in the morning," she says, "but I don't care how many times I have it. Every time a big snow come, I get a taste for snow ice cream. I guess you never outgrow it."

"I hope I don't," I say, putting the first spoonful of this delicious, rich ice cream on my tongue. "I don't know why the ice-cream makers don't just shovel up all the snow first thing and keep it in freezers all year. All they have to add is milk and sugar and flavoring and they got the best ice cream they can make."

"Sounds easy, but I guess it ain't," says Sweetmama.

The ice cream is colder than regular ice cream. I don't know why. And it tastes good when you're eating

it, but after a while my forehead begins to hurt from
the cold and the back of my throat feels raw.

Sweetmama gives a little cough. "This is sure cold, but it's worth it."

It takes us a long time to climb through the snow to church, and when we get near, we hear the choir singing.

"We must be late," says Mother.

"Blame it on the ice cream," says my grandmother.

Mother sends me to the Sunday-school cloakroom to take off my galoshes and hang up my coat. "Don't be long. Service already started," she whispers.

I'm happy to see my girl friends, Shirley and Audrey, just taking off their coats. Shirley comes over and grabs my hand. "We were worried, thinking you weren't coming because of the snow," she says.

"Everybody except the choir and Reverend Hovis is late," Audrey says.

We sit down on the rug in the cloakroom and talk for a minute.

"What you think, Bob, you going to join the church and be baptized at Easter like Audrey and me?" Shirley asks.

I just love Shirley. She's got long eyelashes and a soft heart. She's the only girl I wish I was like. Her voice is high and soft, and she never screams like I do when I'm mad or when I just feel like being loud, and she's got skinny legs and little tiny feet. She doesn't look very tough, because to tell the truth, she's kind of skinny all over, but if anybody messes around with me, she's ready to fight. I love her, but when she starts talking about getting baptized, my heart gives a thump and I wish she would just shut up about it. I've been trying to forget that I got to decide whether I'm going to do it or not.

"You going to?" asks Audrey.

"I don't know. It's a lot of responsibility being baptized. You got to try to watch what you do and what you say, trying to be a good person. It may be too much for me. Maybe I just can't do it. Always be trying; always be failing. That can make you real tired."

"You going to be a hundred and fifty before you think you perfect enough to get baptized," says Audrey.

"You think you perfect enough now?" I ask her.

"Of course."

"You don't have to act so stuck up about it," I tell her. "Who you think you are, Bette Davis?"

"I know one thing I am," she says. "I am ready to be baptized like all the other kids around here except you. Nobody turns ten without being baptized. It's the thing to do."

Lucky I got Shirley to be my best friend. Audrey's too hankty-acting for me sometimes.

When we get ready to go upstairs, Audrey sees Joyce Brown going up the basement steps ahead of us. Without another word to us she runs and catches up with her. That's why sometimes I don't like Audrey. One minute she's acting like she's our friend, the next minute she's running up behind somebody else and forgetting she ever knew us. Shirley's been my friend, my best

friend, ever since we were little; too young to talk.
When I'm feeling bad, it makes her feel bad, and when she's sad, I get low myself.

Shirley and I sit together during the church service, and we cut our eyes at Audrey. She's sitting on the other side of the church with that Joyce Brown who Audrey thinks is so fine because she's got big round muscles in her legs from jumping hot peppers morning, noon, and night.

All through the service I think about Shirley and Audrey getting up at the revival meeting and declaring themselves ready to be baptized. How do they know they are ready? Don't they get into trouble? Don't they tell lies sometimes? Would they sneak and take a horse and hide him without telling anybody?

I smell something smell like grape perfume. The ushers are passing around Communion in tiny glasses filled with grape juice, look like rubies in the light. I have always wanted to taste that Communion drink, supposed to be wine like Jesus' blood. Ever since I've been coming to church, my mouth has watered every first Sunday as they pass the Communion from pew to pew and some people take a glass and tiny piece of crumbled-up soda cracker, supposed to be God's body. But you have to be baptized and taken care of all of your sins before you can have Communion. I'd almost get baptized so I could taste that juice I been drooling over all these years. But are all of these people taking Communion free of their sins? If they are, how did they get that way?

Church service is almost over when Reverend Hovis raises his hand in benediction, and everybody stands. "May the Lord bless you and keep you, may He put His hands upon you in everlasting peace. Amen."

Then everybody sings "Blessed be the tie that bindeth with love," and it's over. We go downstairs for church supper, and I can't wait until it's over, but Mother and Sweetmama take a long time—forever, it seems to me —saying good-bye, shaking hands and hugging people and calling them sugar and sweetheart.

Chuckie is waiting in the hallway when we get home. "Hi, Mrs. Weathers," he says. "Can Bob come over and help me tie up some papers? My boy-scout troop collected them for the paper war drive."

"I guess so, Chuckie. She just have to come upstairs first and change out of those Sunday clothes."

I change quick and pull on my old skirt and sweater and put some pants on too.

"Now, Chuckie, you walk Bob back before dark, you hear?" says Mother.

"I will, Mrs. Weathers," says Chuckie, pulling me quick by the hand and down the stairs.

"We got to go over my house first," he says. "My mother thinks we are going to be in the basement tying up all of those newspapers. So we got to pretend to go down there for a while."

"You children be careful in that basement," says Mrs. Williams when we get to Chuckie's. "I'll be taking a nap."

Mrs. Williams works at the same defense plant making supplies for the army, only she works from mid-
night to eight in the morning, and my mother works
during the day.

"You stay by yourself when your mother goes to
work?" I ask Chuckie.

"Just started. Before, always got to go to my aunt's
house. Now that I'm ten, she thinks I can take care of
myself."

"You're lucky. I'm the only one left that's got to
have somebody take care of me."

"Sometimes it's lucky, but it's not so good when I
wake up and it's still dark and there's nobody but me,"
he says, opening the door to the basement and feeling
around for the light.

We stay in the basement for a half-hour. I show
Chuckie the *Black Beauty* book that tells how Black
Beauty was first hitched to a wagon.

"You smart to bring this," says Chuckie, grabbing it
from me. "I don't know how to hitch up a horse."

I wait in the basement while Chuckie tiptoes upstairs
and gets our coats and galoshes.

We put them on in a hurry. "My mother was asleep.
She didn't hear a thing."

It's getting dark outside, and the snow is beginning
to fall again. We hear a *ping, ping* sound like music,
but it's only the ice cracking on the branches of the
trees and the bushes.

When we get to Yoki's Grocery Store, we see the
second-floor windows are all lit up where Mr. Straus-

burger lives. But the store is closed, and the front-door shade is pulled down.

It takes two of us to push open the side yard gate, there's so much snow around the bottom.

Lucky the snow is deep, because nobody can hear us walking around.

"Suppose somebody look down out the window?" I ask.

"Now, why they do that?" asks Chuckie, leaping over the snow to Yoki's shed. First we quick take as much hay and oats as we can and put it in the wagon.

"He got to have something to eat until we can get back to him," says Chuckie.

It's hard work wading through all of that snow and lifting the hay, going back and forth for what seems like a hundred times.

"That's enough, Chuckie. We got to hurry. It's getting dark, and I'm supposed to be back home before dark. I don't want my mother to start looking for me. She might see us with Yoki."

Chuckie brought his boy-scout flashlight, and we keep having to look at the *Black Beauty* book while we try to get Yoki's harness on and hitch him up to the wagon.

"This is not easy," says Chuckie.

"You right about that," I say.

It gets darker and darker. Lucky for the snow, it never gets pitch-black. Like Mother say, the snow makes everything bright.

Finally we do it. I *slosh, slosh* as fast as I can over to the gate and push both sides wide open so Chuckie can lead Yoki out.

The wheels of the wagon and Yoki's hooves make almost no sound because of the thick soft snow.

When we lead him out to the street, Chuckie says, "Let's take turns driving."

"Do you know how to drive?" I ask.

"No, but can't be too hard," he says. He gives the reins a pull and says real quiet, "Giddap." Yoki starts off with a jerk, and we look at each other and smile.

"Now all we got to do is stay on this street for eight blocks, then turn right toward the river, go a block and then cross the railroad tracks and then start going downhill until we come to the shack," Chuckie says.

I can't help but think how lucky we are that we know every part of the riverfront near our neighborhood from playing down there so much in the summertime. It's the best place to catch grasshoppers, to pick giant sunflowers, and to find hideouts. Also to sit on the bank and watch the riverboats go up and down the Mississippi.

We go about a block when Yoki turns left onto Mayberry Street.

"Yoki, no, you're supposed to go straight!" says Chuckie, pulling back on the reins so hard, he's standing on the back of his heels.

But Yoki doesn't pay him any mind and keeps going up Mayberry Street. All of a sudden he stops.

"What's wrong with this horse?" asks Chuckie. "If we don't get back on that street, somebody's going to see us and make us take him back."

"Go, Yoki, go!" I scream.

"Don't talk so loud," Chuckie tells me.

But Yoki just stands there. I get out and go up to him and try to look him in the eye. "Yoki, you crazy or something? You going to the glue factory if you don't start up." I try pulling him, but he won't budge.

I hop back in to tell Chuckie, and I almost fall down because Yoki gives a jerk, and we're off again.

"How we going to get him back on the right street?" I ask.

But before Chuckie can answer, Yoki stops again. The snow is coming harder, and it's getting later and later.

"Oh, no," says Chuckie. "You go out there and talk to him!"

I hop out and tell Yoki, "You got to stop this, horse. You got to help yourself. Get going."

I hop back in and he starts off again. Two houses later, he stops.

"Chuckie, you know what this crazy horse is doing?" I say. "He's stopping at the houses he delivers milk to. He knows every stop by heart."

"But he can't do this. We've got to get him out of here!"

I get out again and go over and pull his head down and look him in his eyes. "Yoki, this is an emergency. We are not delivering milk. You do that in the morn-

ing. Can't you see it's dark outside, you old nutty
horse!"

But Yoki still stops, and he won't start until somebody jumps out of the wagon and jumps back in.

"All we can do right now," says Chuckie, sounding like he's going to cry, "is to jump in and out fast so he can go faster. Maybe if we let him finish his deliveries, then he will go where we want him to go."

"But suppose that takes five hours," I say. "Suppose Mr. Strausburger delivers milk to a hundred people."

Just then Yoki turns the corner onto our street, Culpepper.

"Oh, no, we're in trouble now," I say. "In a minute he'll be stopping in front of *my* door!"

"This is a mess," says Chuckie as Yoki stops two houses down from where I live. I look down the street and I see Mrs. Beene out front, putting ashes on the sidewalk in front of the house even though it's still snowing. "I'll be right back, Chuckie. I got to talk to Mrs. Beene!"

Mrs. Beene looks up when she sees me trying to run fast through the snow. "Mrs. Beene, you've got to help us!" I say.

"We've got Yoki and we're trying to get him to a hiding place, but he wouldn't go where we want him to go. He thinks he's supposed to deliver milk and he just started off going where he always goes."

Mrs. Beene puts down her bucket of ashes and looks up the street where I'm pointing. And then she does a surprising thing. A big grin goes up the sides of her face, and then she makes a bubbling sound way down in her throat, and next I hear a giggle and then she starts to laugh.

"Shhhh, Mrs. Beene, please, my mother or grandmother will hear you."

I have never seen her smile, let alone heard her laugh. She laughs so hard, she slaps her forehead, and then she sits down in the snow and laughs some more.

"Mrs. Beene, please."

Finally she gets up and she crunches over the ashes two houses down to where the milk wagon is. She takes a good look at Yoki and runs her hand over the dip in his back. She gets down and looks at his legs and his hooves. She walks around the front and looks him over. She pats his nose. "Good horse," she says, and then she looks very serious.

"Where you taking him?"

"Over to the riverfront, Mrs. Clay's old house," Chuckie says.

Mrs. Beene doesn't look at us like she thinks it's a crazy idea. She just gives a nod and climbs into the wagon, and I run quick and get in because Yoki's starting off again. She takes the reins from Chuckie and makes a few clicking sounds on the roof of her mouth with her tongue and snaps the reins, and Yoki lifts his head like he heard somebody say something and starts to move off faster than I've ever seen him.

Mrs. Beene turns Yoki onto the right street, and we go as fast as we can in the snow.

"Lucky so much snow," Mrs. Beene says. "Nobody
see ya."

"Yes, ma'am" is all I can say. I'm so happy.

The black-and-white gates go down and the lights
flash red as we get to the railroad crossing. We have to
stop while a long passenger train with yellow light coming from the windows passes by.

We bump over the tracks after the train is gone and
then down a hill and around a corner, and there is Mrs.
Clay's shack still standing. We unhitch Yoki, and Mrs.
Beene leads him to the shack. Lucky it's old and the
front's all broken down, because we just have to pull
off some wood hanging down where the door used to be
and we make an opening big enough for Yoki to go
through. We work fast putting in the hay and the oats,
and Mrs. Beene ties Yoki to an old iron wood stove
where Mrs. Clay used to bake us tea cakes when I was
five, before she moved away to live with her daughter
in Detroit. There is still newspapers on the wall, but
nothing else is left except the stove.

"Now you got a good home, Yoki," says Chuckie.
"Nobody's going to take you to the glue factory."

"How you going to take care of him?" asks Mrs.
Beene.

"We going to come every day after school and bring
him some oats and walk him around a little," I say.

She looks down at us with that big V between her
eyes like she is saying, "Now, where you two going to
get hay and oats?" But she doesn't say it, of course. I

guess she's almost used up all the words she's going to say today.

"What we going to do with the wagon?" asks Chuckie.

"Let's hide it on the side of the house for now," I say. "Maybe later we think of something to do with it."

All of us pull the wagon to the side of the house where nobody can see it coming down toward the river and nobody can see it from the river where the boats floating on.

"This is where Mrs. Clay used to plant her tomatoes and collards," I say. Coming down here to Mrs. Clay's has made me really miss her. I don't like for people I like a lot to leave. I just try not to think about it.

We get Yoki's blanket out of the wagon, and Mrs. Beene puts it over him. "Good-bye, Yoki," I say. "We'll see you tomorrow."

Mrs. Beene, Chuckie, and I walk back in the snow falling heavy. It's only six blocks to our house, but it seems like it takes a long time. I'm getting so I'm tired of snow. I've been walking around in it all day, and it's been hard to do. All I want is to get home and get into bed with my rabbit, Rose.

We walk past Chuckie's house first, and we whisper good night to him. "That's all right. My mother's sleeping," he says. "I got to go and tie up those newspapers so she won't ask me what I was doing if I wasn't tying them up."

Mrs. Beene and I take off our galoshes and put them

near the front door. I look up at Mrs. Beene, and she stares down at me, looking as mean as ever. I throw my arms around her waist. "You a good friend to me," I say.

She doesn't answer, just hugs me back and then pushes me away and goes to her door. All her cats follow behind her like they in a parade.

When I get upstairs, Sweetmama is sewing at the kitchen table.

"Where you been so late? It's after dark."

"I stopped to talk to Mrs. Beene."

"You and that landlady. Ain't never seen nothin' like it," she says.

I start to yawn, I'm so tired. "Where's my mother?"

"She's working tonight. Got some rush on at the plant. Seem like can't never make enough to satisfy this war. Guns, jeeps, clothes, bullets, you name it."

I yawn again.

"How come you so tired? Ain't done nothin' today but go to church, eat supper, and tie up some newspapers. Maybe you get so tired, you and that landlady yakking away downstairs."

I can't tell her why I'm tired. For a minute I wish I could. But I can't. I never can. I just throw my arms around her neck and put my head on her shoulder and fall right to sleep.

7

THE MYSTERIOUS DISAPPEARANCE

"Funny thing, no milk come this morning," my grandmother says as I hurry up and put on my galoshes. I want to visit Yoki before I go to school.

"Guess old man Strausburger's nephew slow learning the rounds. Course, I don't see why; that old horse know every stop on the road."

I wonder what my grandmother would say if she knew Chuckie and I took Yoki and hid him. I don't say a thing about the milk delivery. I just quick put on my coat and red wool hat my grandmother got at the rummage sale Saturday and washed out for me to wear.

"Oh, before I forget, your mama gave me this note for you before she left for work this morning. She said she found it slipped under the door."

My name is printed on a white folded piece of paper. I open the note and it says: BOB, FEED THE CATS TODAY. MRS. BEENE.

"Now, where you think she's off to," my grandmother says, reading the note over my shoulder. "You so early with all that hurrying you been doing, you got plenty of time to go down there and feed all of those cats."

Most of the time I like the job of feeding the cats when Mrs. Beene is away, but today I really hate that I have to do it. That won't give me much time for Yoki.

"See you this evening, Sweetmama," I say to my grandmother as I run down the stairs. "I'll feed them quick and then I'll go."

"Whatchoo in such a hurry for? School be there this Monday morning like it always is. It ain't going no-where," she says, and then goes back into the kitchen and closes the door.

Mrs. Beene always leaves the cat food in a little closet under the stairs. I pull out a big bowl covered with paper and a rubber band around it. Inside is some chicken and mashed-up fish. I don't have time to play with the cats. Just feed them and give them some water in their dish and run out the door and fast up the street to Chuckie's house.

His mother raises the window and looks out when I ring the bell.

"Chuckie ready?"

"He's coming right down, Bob. My, you two becoming good friends. Just don't let Chuckie start you in his mischievous ways," and then she quick pulls down the window because it's cold outside.

"We got to go quick and feed Yoki," I tell Chuckie when he comes out carrying his knapsack over one shoulder.

We don't talk much on the way to the river. The wind is so cold, it gives me a headache.

When we are facing the river, the wind is worse, and we have to bend our heads down and wrap our neck scarves around our noses and mouths and pull our caps down just above our eyebrows so all that's showing are our eyes.

We cross the railroad tracks and start down the hill toward Mrs. Clay's shack and Yoki. When we come close to the shack, we stop and stare. We can't believe our eyes.

"The wagon's gone!" says Chuckie.

I run to the shack to check on Yoki, but when I get there, he's gone too. The only thing left is some hay and oats and that wood-burning stove.

"Oh, no," groans Chuckie. "Somebody took Yoki and the wagon. Who could've done it?"

"I wonder where he is," I say. "I feel like he's my horse. I don't know what I'm going to do not knowing what's happening to him."

I run around the side of the house and check just in case Yoki is out there, but he isn't. When I come back

around where Chuckie is, he's walking very slow toward
the house, looking down.

"Whatchoo doing?" I ask.

"We've got to find that horse."

"But how you going to find him looking down like that?"

"I'm tracking."

"Tracking?"

"Like Tonto. Looking for footprints and then reading them."

"Chuckie, this isn't a movie, this is for real. Yoki's been stolen, and we're to blame for bringing him here."

"Yeah, but if we hadn't brought him here, he'd be on his way to the glue factory."

"Maybe he is anyway. Maybe Mr. Strausburger's nephew found him and brought him back. Maybe he followed our tracks, and if he did that, he'll know that we did it."

"How's he going to do that?" says Chuckie.

"Because he'll see my tracks getting out of the wagon and going to my house and then he'll see my tracks and Mrs. Beene's coming back to the wagon and then the wagon-wheel tracks coming here."

"He can't do that. Because it was snowing last night when we took Yoki, remember? And the snow covered up the tracks. So whoever took Yoki took him after the snow stopped."

I start to help him follow the footprints. "There are horse prints and a person's shoe prints coming from the shack," he says. "Let's just follow them and see where they go."

"Right to the wagon—or where it used to be," I say.

"Somebody hitched up Yoki and then drove off with him," Chuckie says as we follow the wheel tracks back up the hill and across the railroad tracks. We're so worried about Yoki, it doesn't seem cold anymore.

We go across the railroad tracks following the wheel prints, and then when we get to the main street, Broadway, we see that the wagon tracks turn right, and then there are too many other car tracks to tell which is which.

"Whoever took Yoki turned right instead of left toward the store, so it couldn't be Roger Strausburger," I tell Chuckie.

"Well, then, who else?"

"Maybe a factory worker came early and saw the wagon and Yoki and took them. I don't know of any other people come around there," I say.

"Well, somebody did, and they should be put in jail for stealing that horse."

"Then shouldn't we be put in jail because we took him first?"

"But we had to take him to save his life. That's different from just up and stealing something because you want it," says Chuckie.

"You right about that," I say, grabbing his hand. "Come on, Chuckie, I see a streetcar. If we don't catch this one, we'll be late for school, and then the teacher

will write a note home, and everybody will want to
know why we couldn't get to school on time."

"You talking about trouble, then we would have some trouble," says Chuckie as we climb on the street-car just slid to a stop.

As we walk all the way to the back of the streetcar, I can't help but think that no matter if I do something that starts out fine, it always turns into trouble.

We don't say much riding to school. We're in too much trouble to talk. When we get there, Chuckie goes upstairs to his fifth-grade class and I go to my third. When I get there, Shirley looks at me as if to say, "You late. How come?" I'm so low, I don't even cross my fingers on my right hand and hold them up for her to see, which means, "I'll tell you later."

Mrs. Long is standing at her desk, and when I come in, she gives a little frown. "Barbara, don't disturb the class. Just go into the cloakroom and take off your coat and boots and go quietly to your desk."

When I tiptoe to my desk, she is holding up a little book and talking about buying war bonds. "Every time you buy a stamp for a quarter, you paste it in your book," she says. "When this book is all filled up, you can turn it in to me and you will get a war bond." Then she passes out the books and tells us all to do the best we can.

Next two monitors help Mrs. Long pass out new red, white, and blue songbooks. I love the smell of new books, and I pick mine up and open it to pages never been used before and put the book up to my face and take a big sniff. It makes me feel a little better.

"Class," Mrs. Long says, "these are all American songs written by American composers. Who knows what a composer is?"

Nobody raises a hand. Then a few kids turn around and look at me. They always do that. Everybody think I know everything, especially if they don't know it.

"Turn around, please," says Mrs. Long. "Barbara, can you help us out?"

"He writes music," I say very quietly.

"He can be a she too," says Mrs. Long.

Then she tells us to turn to the songs under "Patriotic." "Now I want somebody to go to the dictionary and look up the word *patriotic* and tell us what it means."

Usually I try to beat out everybody, raising my hand first even before the teacher finish asking the question, but today I just sit there, and she calls on Shirley to look up the word.

"Let's correct that," says Mrs. Long. "Shirley, the word you look up first should be *patriotism*."

" 'Love and loyal support of one's own country.' "

"Thank you, Shirley. These songs tell of love and loyalty to America, our country. There are some we already know or we've heard, especially since we've been fighting to protect our country, and others that you might not have heard."

She goes over to the piano and starts to play "America the Beautiful," and we sing along. Everybody sings very loud and strong when we come to the part at the

end, and Mrs. Long bangs hard on the piano and leans
back and throws her head back and sings, but I just
mumble a little. My heart's not in it.

Then she asks us to turn to page 33. "Now, class,"
she says, "I am not going to teach you some of these
songs. Any that are derogatory about black people,
colored people, we won't sing them. I don't know what
the composers were thinking about when they wrote
them, but that's their problem, not ours.

"I want you especially to take this page and fold it
over. The song is called, as you see, 'Old Black Joe.'
The composer, Stephen Foster, wrote some beautiful
tunes, but some of the songs were not right," she says,
wiggling her nose like something don't smell right.

Everybody been slouching sit up straight and start
going through the pages trying to see if there were some
more Stephen Foster songs that were derogatory.

"What does *derogatory* mean, Mrs. Long?" asks
Audrey.

"Each of you think about it all through lunch, and
when we come back, I want you to write down what
you think it is."

Everybody groans and cuts dirty looks at Audrey.
Why did she have to open her big mouth. All I want to
do is go home and sit in the thinking chair in the bathroom with Rose.

It's very cold outside, and Mrs. Long tells us we
can play in the room after we eat our lunch. So we get
out games and books and we sit on the floor all around
the room, having fun.

"I'm not leaving anybody in charge because everybody is in charge of themselves," Mrs. Long tells us. She takes her lunch and goes down the hall to have lunch with Mrs. Watkins, who is the principal of the school.

As soon as she leaves, somebody says, "Let's get that songbook out and see if we can find out how that song she don't want us to sing sounds."

Everybody thinks this is a good idea, even me, and I don't think much is a good idea today.

Joyce Brown's the only one can play the piano, and she rolls up the stool and somebody holds the page open for her while she picks out the tune.

We listen carefully, and the third time we start to hum it, looking down at our songbooks. The fourth time we start to sing the words, "I'm coming, I'm coming, for my . . ."

"I'm shocked!" says Mrs. Long, standing in the doorway with her hands on her hips and a big frown on her face. "Back to your seats. Looks like I haven't made myself very clear about a song like 'Old Black Joe.' "

We go and sit down. My stomach gives a jump. I don't like how mad she is. She is usually almost perfect, and I want to be just like her when I grow up and make something of myself.

"Now, class, we have talked about this, and you know all about slavery and how colored people were forced to do hard work in this country and not be paid for it. They had to do it or be killed, or they were afraid their families would be killed, because there wasn't many of them over here at the time and they couldn't defend themselves. If there was a slave named Joe, we don't need to hear a song about him unless it's a song praising him for the work that he did in building this country and condemning how hard he was forced to work. This song does not do that, and we will not sing it!"

"We're sorry, Mrs. Long," says Shirley. "Me too, me too," say other children. We all feel sorry that we made Mrs. Long mad.

"Instead of a sentence or two on the word *derogatory*, I want you to write an essay and give me examples of situations that you think could be derogatory."

I wish that we had never heard of Stephen Foster and "Old Black Joe." This day is never going to end.

8

BOB MAKES A DECISION

I'm the first one out the door when the last bell rings, and I go right upstairs and wait outside Chuckie's room. I don't wait for Shirley and I know it's going to hurt her feelings, but I can't sit with her on the streetcar like we always do. I've got to talk to Chuckie.

"Maybe we should stop by Yoki's Grocery. Maybe they heard something about Yoki," I say as we walk out of school.

"I don't know if that's a good idea," he says. "I think we just should stay away from there."

Chuckie and I ride in the back on the way home.

Everybody turning around looking at us. They are sur- :83
prised. We're supposed to be blood enemies. Shirley
gets on with Audrey and she looks back where we're
already sitting down and she looks like her feelings are
really hurt. Audrey cuts her eyes at me as if to say,
"What you sitting with that mean old Chuckie boy
for?" But I pretend I don't see a thing. They don't
know that Chuckie and I have a secret together that's a
terrible secret and we need to sit together.

We get off at our stop and wave at Mr. Jenkins
standing in the window of the bake shop. "Well, you
going to go with me into Yoki's?" I ask, starting toward
the grocery store.

"I don't want to, but if you're going to do it, I might
as well. I'm braver than you any day."

"You crazy," I say, poking out my lip. "Nobody is
braver than me."

We go inside and pretend to be looking around at
the cans on the shelves.

"Well, what you two kids want?" Roger says like
he's very angry about something.

"Hi, Roger," says Chuckie.

"Hi," I say, but it doesn't come out loud because my
throat feels dry, I'm so scared.

"We come in to ask if it's all right to bring in some
newspapers we collected for the paper drive," says
Chuckie.

"Do what you want," says Roger, frowning and bending over some papers on the counter. "Just don't
bother me, got enough to worry about."

"What . . . what's wrong?" I ask, and it sounds like my voice is shaking.

"Everything is wrong!" says Roger, slamming the pencil down on the counter. "Somebody came in here and stole that horse you are so crazy about, and the wagon too!"

"That's . . . that's . . . terrible," says Chuckie, and his voice sounds like it's shaking.

"Terrible! It's worse than that, it's criminal. Stealing is a crime, and whoever did this is going to be put under the jail!"

I grab Chuckie's arm and look at Roger with big eyes.

"In the old days out West, stealing a horse was the worst thing you could do. You know what happened to horse thieves?"

"What?" we ask together real soft.

"They hanged them!"

We don't say a thing, just stand there holding each other's hands.

"What do they do now to horse thieves?" I ask.

"Put them in jail and throw away the key, I hope."

"Who would want to steal Yoki?" Chuckie says.

"I don't know. All I know is that it beat me out of a hundred thirty-five dollars. I was selling that old mangy horse for thirty-five dollars and the wagon for a hundred. So somebody stole a hundred thirty-five dollars from me, and I hope the police catch whoever did it real soon."

"The police know about it?" asks Chuckie in a little voice.

"Darn right they do. Nobody comes around here and steals a hundred thirty-five dollars right out of my pocket."

"Oh," Chuckie and I say together.

"We got to go," says Chuckie.

"Bring those newspapers in, but like I said, don't disturb me. Too bad you're out of a horse to visit, but you wouldn't have been seeing him anyway. The truck came an hour ago, and if I had still had that horse, he woulda been on his way to becoming glue," he says and gives that laugh of his.

"I'm still glad we did it," I say when we get outside.

"Me too. I just hope Yoki isn't sold to the glue factory by whoever stole him," says Chuckie.

"And I hope nobody finds out we took that horse. I'm too young to go to jail."

"You won't be put in jail, just in reform school."

"You kiddin' me."

"I'm not. I know somebody was put in there for running away from home."

"Just only for that?"

"So you know if you steal something, you going to go."

I say good-bye to Chuckie and walk slowly up the stairs to our house. Now I got to worry about being put in jail or reform school.

After I eat my snack, I go out with Rose to the hall

bathroom and curl up in the big armchair. I've got a lot of thinking to do. I don't think it's right to put somebody in jail who does something so someone won't be killed. I try to think some more about Yoki and that Roger at the store, but I'm too sleepy. I tuck Rose under my head and fall asleep.

When I wake up, Mrs. Walker is leaning in the doorway. "Barbara, wake up, dear. I've got to use the bathroom."

"Oh, hi, Mrs. Walker," I say, looking at the big stack of magazines she's carrying. I know she just wants to sit in this chair, but I guess it's not fair for me to have it so long.

I go into the kitchen and tell Sweetmama that I'm going downstairs to see the cats.

When I go down the stairs, I see Mrs. Beene taking the flag back outside. "Mrs. Beene, I fed the cats like you wanted," I say.

She finishes propping up the flag and yawns. She opens her mouth very wide and yawns and then she remembers to put her hand over her mouth halfway through.

It seems strange to see her yawning. I never thought of her sleeping or being sleepy, she's so busy cleaning all the time.

She yawns two more times. She yawns so hard, I see two tears at the corners of her eyes. Then she looks down at me and says, "Don't be sad."

"How you know I'm sad, Mrs. Beene?" I ask.

She just smile at me without answering. I follow her

inside and into her kitchen, where she puts the cookie
jar in the middle of the table and starts making me
some lemon tea with a slice of onion in it.

"Mrs. Beene, I'm in a lot of trouble," I say, too worried to eat a cookie. "Roger at the store says the police
are looking for who stole Yoki and when they're found
they're going to be put in jail and something worse than
that happened this morning. Chuckie and I went to
feed Yoki and somebody had stolen him and the
wagon," I say, beginning to cry.

Mrs. Beene sets the tea down in front of me and she
says in a soft voice, "I took him."

I'm too surprised to say anything. Mrs. Beene looks
like she thinks the way I'm looking at her so surprised
is funny, and she's going to burst out laughing. But she
doesn't. She sits down and stirs her tea and says, "He's
at my farm in Vidalia."

"You mean, you took Yoki?"

"Got up middle of the night soon's snow stopped
fallin'. Been driving him the rest o' the night and then I
had to take the bus back. Tired. Can't sleep on no
buses. Drive too fast for me."

"But, Mrs. Beene, why did you take him? Chuckie
and me, we been scared and worried all day not knowing what happened to Yoki."

"Don't want you to get in trouble."

"But we weren't going to get in trouble."

She thinks a minute before she talks again, like she's
wondering whether she can stand to talk so much at
one time, and then she says, "Last night 'twas too late

to turn around. Roger would see the wagon coming back, probably. You and the boy would get in trouble. Better to keep on going."

"But we thought you helped us because you didn't think it was right to kill Yoki."

"I don't."

"But you said—"

"Don't think it's right for you to get in trouble for doing what's right, either."

"But if you think that . . ."

"You and the boy can't take care of no horse," she says, looking me straight in the eye like what she's saying is right and no need for me to say it's wrong.

"We could get oats and hay to take care of him," I say, but I start to feel like she's right.

"Where from?"

"Well . . ." I say, feeling embarrassed.

"You get the doctor, he get sick?"

"Well . . . I guess . . ." And then I think of something that makes me feel sick to my stomach. "Mrs. Beene, if Roger finds out you have Yoki, you could go to jail."

"Ain't nobody going to jail."

"But you don't know Roger. He'd probably like to see you in jail so he can brag about it. He's terrible!"

She acts like she doesn't hear me. "If it ever come up, I'll say I took the horse."

"But we took Yoki, not you. It's not fair for you to take the blame for Chuckie and me."

"Don't worry about something haven't happened yet."

"Suppose they find out?"

She just yawns some more and gets up. "Got to go lie down. Ain't slept a wink."

I go to the door as Mrs. Beene keeps on yawning and wiping the tears out of her eyes. She really looks tired.

I don't want to ask her this question because I'm scared of what she's going to say, but I do anyway. "Mrs. Beene?" She looks down at me while holding the door open. "If we could have turned around and taken Yoki back and you thought Roger wouldn't find out, would you have taken him back?"

"It was his horse," she says. Before I can say anything, she starts to close the door. "Come again."

I feel my heart cracking all up inside. Even Mrs. Beene would have let Yoki be killed just because he belongs to Roger. I can't believe it. I don't want to believe it, but it's true.

My grandmother is sitting at the kitchen table reading a *Life* magazine when I come in.

"You leave early this morning, you come home late after school."

"I stopped at Mrs. Beene's."

"You and that landlady. What happens down there? You talk a mile a minute, she don't say nothing at all?"

"She gave me some cookies." I take off my coat and head for the other room to change into my play clothes.

"And here I fixed you some hot corn muffins and fresh buttermilk."

"That's all right, I'll eat that too," I tell her because I don't want to hurt her feelings. After what Mrs.

Beene just told me, it's going to be hard to stuff that food down. I feel so bad, maybe I'll never eat again.

"In a little while I got to go over to the church," Sweetmama says. "My committee is planning what quartets and choirs going to be invited to the revival."

"Oh," I say in a little voice. I don't want to even think about any revival and especially not about joining the church and getting baptized. I'm so far from being ready for that. I'm closer to being put in jail.

"What's the matter with you?" my grandmother asks, putting down her magazine.

"Sweetmama, when did you know you were ready to get baptized?"

"When I thought I could put away my childish ways and know right from wrong."

I go over and sit on her lap. "I'm all mixed up. Sometimes I feel like I don't know what I'm doing even thinking about getting baptized."

"Ain't you ready to start growing up? When you going to start, you don't start now?"

I just shrug.

"When I was a girl and time come to decide whether we going to get baptized, it was the thing to do in the country to send the child off by theyself to think about it," says my grandmother, giving me a hug. I just lay my head back on her shoulder, get ready to hear about the old days. They're the best stories I ever heard, and they're true too.

"I didn't eat anything and I didn't drink anything

until the sun went down, 'cause that's what you had to
do. But lucky it was winter, just before spring, and that
sun went down about five o'clock, because I got so
thirsty, thought I wasn't going to make it." She laughs
and I give a giggle.

"I went off to the woods and I just thought to myself,
What is this baptizing all about? I also saw some squir-
rels and rabbits and took time off from all that heavy
thinking to see if I could tip up on them and catch me
one. I couldn't eat *then*, but maybe I could bring something back to eat *later*.

"Anyway, when I could, I thought about that baptizing. Could I follow the Ten Commandments? I saw
grown people every day breaking those commandments
—couldn't follow them if they life depended on it.
What made me think I could? Finally I just said to
myself, 'Josie, you going to do the best you can in life.
You know right from wrong and you going to try to do
right. You just do your best.'"

"That's all you had to decide? To do the best you
could?"

"Always doing the best you can is a hard thing to do.
It sounds easy, but it ain't."

I give a sigh and slide off her lap. "You lucky you
could decide like that," I say.

"I knew I wouldn't be perfect, but who is?" she says,
picking up her magazine again.

I sat up straight when I heard that. She's right. Nobody is perfect, let alone me.

"But how could you be responsible for all the things you did good or bad when you were only eight years old?" I ask her.

"Who else is supposed to be responsible for something you've done if you know right from wrong?"

"Nobody?" I say, real quiet. "But suppose somebody else wants to take the blame for something you did even though you don't want them to?"

"Nobody can take the blame for something you did unless you let them," she says, getting up and starting to clash two butcher knives together to sharpen them so she can cut up some salt pork.

I get to the streetcar stop early the next morning and bounce up and down in the cold, waiting for Chuckie. I tell him what happened to Yoki as soon as I see him.

"You're kiddin' me," he says.

"No, Mrs. Beene's got him out on her farm in Vidalia."

"Why'd she do it?"

"Because she said we couldn't take care of him, and somebody might find out."

"We could have taken care of him," he says.

"I think she's right, Chuckie. We'd have to have somebody adopt him quick, and suppose no one did?"

"Well . . . maybe so, but—"

"The only bad part is she wants to take all the blame even if somebody finds out."

"What's bad about that?"

"Chuckie!"

We can't talk anymore because the streetcar comes, and Shirley keeps slapping the seat beside her for me to sit down. I try to raise my eyebrows at Chuckie to say, "I'll talk more later."

Shirley and I stay inside out of the cold and play jacks in the back of the class at lunchtime. We play a lot together in school because we don't get to visit too much in the wintertime. It gets dark early, and we live twenty blocks away from each other.

"You going to do it?" asks Shirley.

"I can't do it, Shirley. I just can't."

"I wanted the three of us to join the church and get baptized together," she says, looking like she's going to cry.

"Something's happened. I just can't do it."

"But what happened?"

"I can't tell you."

"You can tell me. I'm your best friend . . . or I was until that old Chuckie started hanging around you."

"You're still my best friend," I tell her. "All I can say is if I get baptized, I'd be pretending I'm a better person than I am. I did something, and somebody else will take the blame if the secret comes out, because I'm scared to tell anybody I did it."

"Do you want this person to take the blame for you?"

"Oh, no. I wish this person never would have said she'd take the blame on herself. I wish she'd never heard of what I did."

"See, you got a good heart and that's what counts. You can't help it if you're scared to take the blame."

"My grandmother said that nobody can take the blame for something I did unless I let them. I'm supposed to try to do the best I can in life, and that's not the best I can do."

Shirley thinks about this. She's trying hard to put this in a good light. That's what I like about her—she always tries to look on the good side of things. Me, I'm looking at the good, the bad, and the medium all at one time.

"Well, you are doing the best you can, considering how scared you are. The best you can do right now is to worry about the other person taking the blame for you and thinking it's not right."

See what I mean. She makes things sound so much better. It's easy to believe her. "Maybe I am doing the best I can," I tell her.

"It sounds like it to me," she says, poking a candy cane into her sour pickle.

"I'm feeling a little better about everything," I tell her, throwing the jacks out for twosies.

"Then you'll do it."

I look at Shirley, and she looks like she's about to say "Please, please, please, double please."

I can't help it. I start to smile for the first time since Yoki disappeared.

"That means you will!" says Shirley, jumping up.

"Well, I guess I will," I say. My heart gives a thump. Shirley starts to skip around the room, knocking the chalk and the erasers off the blackboard, and then she goes to her desk.

"Whatchoo doing?" I ask.

She comes back over with her notebook and a pencil.

"I'm going to write my daddy right now about you and me getting baptized together," she says. "He's going to like this. Remember how he used to call us the terrible twins?" I giggle when she says that. Her daddy, Leon, could always make me laugh. It's the way he says things.

Shirley's daddy and my daddy are best friends, and they used to listen to the ball game together every Saturday at our house. Shirley's mother never came because Shirley's parents are divorced, but her father takes care of her on Saturdays and Sundays ever since she was a baby. They always stayed for supper when they came over, and her father used to tell my mother, "Saree, you get any better at this cooking, I'm going to turn into the fat man at the circus."

When we'd come back inside from playing in the hall or in the front yard, he'd say, "Here come the terrible twins. What you two got into now?" We'd climb up on our daddies' laps, and they'd let us pour their beer and lick the foam off the top.

"Remember when we all went to the carnival and we had to hold their hands, they got so scared riding with us on the double Ferris wheel?"

"Yeah, and your daddy kept saying, 'Now, girls, don't be scared . . . ain't nothin' to be scared of,'" says Shirley with a giggle.

"Oh, they were funny. I thought my stomach would pop from laughing so hard." We just sit there laughing together, remembering how they were telling us not to be scared and they both had their eyes closed tight, too afraid to look down.

"My mother says when they come home, she's going to fix everything your daddy and my daddy liked the best—all of it—she's saving rationing stamps for it, I bet."

"Won't that be the best," says Shirley, looking off again like she can see it. "Maybe I should start listening to the baseball games, know all about it when they come back."

"Let's do it and surprise them. We'll know about the Brooklyn Dodgers, the Cardinals, the Red Sox. They won't believe it. When your daddy comes back, you think you'll be too big to sit on his lap like we used to?"

Shirley stops smiling. "This war go on a long time, maybe he'll come back won't even know me, I'll be so big."

"You his child. He'll know you no matter how grown up you are when he comes back," I say, but I'm not so sure, now that Shirley brought it up. Suppose my daddy comes home, I open the door and he says, 'My daughter, Bob, she here, miss?' "

"You know one thing I hate?" asks Shirley.

"What?" I say, swallowing down a dry throat trying not to cry.

"One's in the navy and the other's in the army. Ain't right they been friends so long split up like that."

"Must be a reason for it," I tell her. "I asked my

daddy if he ever bumped into your daddy, but he wrote back and said no."

"Wouldn't that been a good thing if they had?" says Shirley, looking off in space like she can see it. "They could have probably listened to a German baseball game together."

"In German?" I ask, looking at her like she's lost her mind.

Shirley starts to laugh, and so do I. "Anyway, they can't do nothing like that without us around. He told me he's glad we still tight friends no matter what," she says.

Just then Audrey comes in from the yard. "What you two grinnin' about?"

We stop smiling and look up at Audrey with big eyes.

"Bob's going to do it. She's going to get baptized on Easter with us," Shirley says. "We can have navy-blue matching Easter outfits from the catalog, with white collars and cuffs."

"Maybe you and me, but Bob's not getting anything new. She never does," says that heifer Audrey.

"You don't know everything, Shorty," I say, getting mad. I'm glad we didn't tell her what we were really grinning about. She'd probably say something mean I'd have to lay her out for.

"I know you don't wear nothing but hand-me-down clothes."

"Whatchoo know about it," I say. I feel like hitting her across the face.

"I know your grandmother gets everything you wear from the rummage sale. Ain't no such thing for you to get something new."

"She does too get something new. She gets things all the time," says Shirley, and I love her for that. That's why she's my best friend and that Audrey is number 2 going on number 142.

"If you tell anybody anything about where I get my clothes," I say, "your name will be mud, because you'll be covered with blood." I wish I could hit Audrey so hard, she'd wake up two weeks from tomorrow. But I can't do it because I have to try to be a better person and stay out of trouble from now on.

What she says is true. Everything I get is a hand-me-down, but it's none of her business.

At supper I tell Sweetmama and Mother that I want to be baptized on Easter Sunday. "You and me sit down every night and read the Scriptures together," says Sweetmama. "When you go in that water be baptized, then you be thinking about the Scriptures. Make your heart ready and then your soul accept."

"Got to get started on your baptizing robe, I guess," says Mother.

"Audrey's making fun of me because I only wear clothes from the rummage sale," I say.

"What's wrong with that?" asks Sweetmama, shaking some tobacco from a little sack into some thin white paper and rolling a cigarette. She holds it with two fingers and licks the edge, and it sticks to itself like magic.

"As long as they good-quality clothes, ain't nothing wrong with it," says Mother.

We don't have much money because everything my mother makes goes in a savings so when the war is over, we will leave Mrs. Beene's rooming house and move to California.

"When we get there," she says all the time, "you going to eat oranges right off the tree and walk to the ocean, reach in, and grab the fish swimming by."

That's why we don't have money for new clothes. Usually I don't mind wearing rummage-sale clothes, but as hard as I try, I can't help but want something new this Easter.

"This is my baptizing Easter," I say to her. "You don't do that but once. Just for once I'd like something new from the mail-order catalog. Shirley and Audrey will have on their outfits, and I just don't think I can stand to see them all dressed up in something new and me in somebody else's clothes," I say.

Mother frowns at me and says, "It's not a good thing to look over and compare what you got to somebody else. Just think of what you have as the best, no matter what it is. The very best. When you look over at somebody else's things and they look better to you, you start feeling smaller and smaller, and that ain't right."

I know it's not right and I really try after that. But I just can't get that outfit out of my mind. The one I want is in the mail-order catalog. The dress is navy blue with white collar and cuffs that come off to be washed and a matching navy-blue coat with two rows of buttons on the front and some white gloves.

Everybody is always dressed to kill on Easter. They go prancing around with their new hats and beautiful new clothes and shiny shoes on. For once I want to be right out there with them.

After school one day I smell corn bread baking in the oven, and my Aunt Talida is there sitting at the table with Mother. Aunt Talida just came back from working in a war plant in Detroit, and Mother took off early from work to meet her at Union Station.

"Come on over here, girl, and give me some sugar," says Aunt Talida. She always says that. She is my favorite aunt. I even like the way one of her eyes shoots off to the side when she supposed to be looking straight ahead.

"She got a weak eye," Mother says, looking sad. "If she had money when she's a girl, doctors could have fixed it. That's where money counts."

I go sit on Aunt Talida's lap and let her kiss me on the cheek.

"That's some good sweet sugar," she says, hugging me tight. She's been saying that since I was young, and it embarrasses me now, but I don't want to hurt her feelings.

Sweetmama comes in carrying a brown bag. It's a St. Matthew's brown bag because it's got a big cross on the front and back.

Sweetmama got that smile on her face like when she thinks she's got something really good. She goes early in the morning every Thursday and Saturday for the rummage and waits outside for the doors to open. "Black and white, we stand together in that line. All of us, we ain't got no money. Nobody studying about being segregated. Just get in there quick and get the best."

Mother loves the clothes Sweetmama brings from St. Matthew's. She says the clothes are in such good shape because the people are so rich who give the clothes. She says they wear everything only once and then buy something new when that gets dirty. "All you have to do is wash these things and it's like *you* wore it once."

Sweetmama is so excited, she don't even take off her coat. She puts the bag she is carrying on the table and says, "Saree, I did it this time!"

She pulls out something pink. Oh, no. Nobody else wears pink but me. Mother hates pink on her, and Sweetmama says she's too old for pink. I never liked pink, either, but that never cut no ice with them.

She holds up this pink dress. Aunt Talida and Mother go "Ooooh" and "Ummmmm."

"Come here, Bob. Let me measure it up against you," says Mother, taking the dress from Sweetmama.

"This is a perfect Easter dress. It's just beautiful."

I don't move.

"Bob, you hear me?"

"I wanted something new," I say, two big tears sitting in my eyes.

"This is better than new," Mother says. "It's got quality. You don't want that old raggedy stuff from the catalog. It falls apart next time you wash it."

I don't care if it falls apart. The important thing is that it's mine first.

"Look at this dress," she says. "It's heavy piqué. I could work three weeks and still not make enough to buy this dress. See, it's got handmade buttonholes down the back, and look at these flowers embroidered at the waist. Ain't never seen nothing like it. Look like they used ten different shades of the same color for the flowers and all the flowers a different color. Who you think sit down and have the patience to do that? This dress is fine; almost too good to wear."

I just stand there staring at the pink thing.

Mother looks at me and she says, "One day you going to know something about quality if it kills me. Now, come here and try on this dress, girl."

I take off my pleated skirt and white blouse, and she slips the dress over my head. It takes a long time to put the buttons in all those handmade buttonholes. When she finishes, she steps back. "It's perfect, just perfect."

"You going to thank me for that pretty dress, Bob?" asks Sweetmama, still standing with her coat on and a cigarette stuck to her bottom lip. She can talk while the cigarette bobs up and down. It never falls off.

I say thank you and just stand there like a brown stick figure.

9

REVIVAL MEETING

The next day Chuckie comes over after his boy-scout meeting. We sit on the top step going up to Mrs. Walker's.

"I still don't see what's so bad about Mrs. Beene taking the blame for taking Yoki if she wants to," says Chuckie.

"You want her to go to jail?"

"No, but I don't want to go to jail, either."

"It's wrong for somebody to take the blame for something you did yourself."

"Nobody knows who took Yoki, so Mrs. Beene hasn't taken the blame yet."

"I'm supposed to be trying to tell the difference between what's right and what's wrong."

"It ain't that easy," says Chuckie. "We took Yoki because it's wrong to kill a horse like that without even trying to find him a new place to live. What we did was right. But if we tell anybody, it'll look like we did wrong because we took a horse that didn't belong to us."

"You're right about that," I say. "The reason Mrs. Beene is taking all the blame is because she thinks we're kids that don't know any better."

"She's right."

"But we do know better," I tell him. "My grandmother is right, though. It sure is hard to always do the best you can."

Every couple of days after that I can't help it but I have to stop at Yoki's Grocery and ask Roger if they've found Yoki, even though I know they haven't.

One day, about a month before Easter, I stop in as usual.

"Back again, huh?" says Roger. "Why do you bother coming to ask about that horse? If I find him, it won't do you any good, because he'll be off to the glue factory before you can reach down and tie your shoelaces," he says, and laughs.

When Roger says things like that, I'm glad we took Yoki. Very glad. I always give a little smile that makes Roger think I think what he's saying is funny, but that little smile is for Yoki, because I can just see him walking around there in the pasture out at Mrs. Beene's,

eating big and then galloping around, or I can see him
in the barn chewing on some hay and humming every
time he thinks of how hard he used to work and how he
doesn't have to work anymore.

"See you, Roger," I say, backing out the door.

"I see you now," he says and gives that laugh that
makes me wish he had pneumonia instead of poor Mr.
Strausburger.

We're all getting ready for the revival meeting, and
I'm nervous because this is the night Audrey, Shirley
and I have to join the church and say we ready to be
baptized.

"Now, sugar, don't be nervous," says Mother, helping me on with my dress. "Revival meeting is lots of
fun. All those choirs coming and singing real loud and
joyous. People be getting happy, and then come that
delicious supper afterward, everybody bring something
good. So much to eat, you don't know what to pick up
first."

"It's going to be hard to get up and sit on the mourner's bench in front of all those people."

"It'll be easy when the time comes," Mother says.

I go into the kitchen and sit down carefully so I
won't wrinkle my dress. Mother calls from the other
room for me to turn off the oven. We're taking a baked
chicken and dressing and a coconut cake to the supper.

I turn it off and sit back down. Sweetmama comes in
from the bathroom and leans over the kitchen sink,
turning up the tips of her hair that show from under-
neath her hat with the hot curling iron. Mother calls to

me again, "Bob, baby, you turn off the stove? I smell something burning."

"Yes, ma'am, I did," I say, going into the other room. I stand behind Mother sitting at the vanity table and watch her put on her makeup.

First she takes a big red rubber sponge, and then she opens up a round box of dark brown powder and she dabs the powder on her forehead, her cheekbones, her chin, and her neck. Next she shakes out the sponge and then uses it to spread the powder all over her face. Her eyebrows disappear and her lips are the same brown color as her face. Then she takes a black pencil with a soft point and makes big curves for eyebrows. Next she rolls up her lipstick, which is the color of maroon crayon and is nice and shiny, and pulls her lips over her teeth and opens her mouth halfway and puts it on. Then she takes most of it off by pressing a tissue on her lips.

"How do I look?" she asks. She always asks me that when I stand by the vanity watching her make up.

"You look real pretty," I say.

She opens a dark blue bottle with a silver label on it called April in Paris perfume and puts two drops behind each ear.

Then I lean over, and she puts some behind my ear, and we smile at each other. But that doesn't last long.

"Saree!" Sweetmama calls from the kitchen. "Come in here. Something's burning in the oven."

We run into the kitchen, and smoke is coming out of the oven. Mother opens it, and a puff of smoke makes

her eyes water, and she starts to cough and close it up
again. She takes a good look at the front of the oven.

"Bob, you turn this all the way up to the top to broil instead of turning it to the right to off. You been turning that oven off for a long time. How you forget this time?"

I just stand there and shrug.

"Girl, I don't know what I'm going to do with you," she says, standing over me with her hands on her hips and her elbows stuck out. That means she's really mad.

The whole kitchen is smoky and smells like burned-up bones. When we get ready to go, Mother picks up the coconut cake. "Guess this all we got to contribute tonight, thanks to Bob."

There's almost no preaching at the revival meeting, which I like. Sometimes Reverend Hovis's preaching goes on so long on Sunday, I feel like I'm going to die and go to heaven before he's through. But tonight there is just lots of singing and holding hands with everybody and clapping. Mrs. Dawson is playing the piano so good, I imagine it's going to start dancing across the floor. A couple of people get so carried away, they do get up and start hopping around.

Shirley, Audrey, and me are sitting together. We're too scared to join in the singing, and we don't even giggle like we used to when people get happy and start throwing up their arms and dancing in the aisles. We just sit with big eyes. Then the time comes and everything quiets down. I begin to sweat, and I have to keep rubbing the palms of my hands on my skirt.

Reverend Hovis gets that heavenly look on his face and lifts his hands and starts singing, "Softly and tenderly, Jesus is calling . . ." And then everybody starts singing it too, real soft. My mother and Shirley and Audrey's mothers turn around on the same pew and give us a nod. That means get up.

"Come on . . . come on . . ." they are singing as I stand up on trembly knees and start toward the mourner's bench. Some other children come up and join too. It seems like my whole Sunday-school class is sitting up there. Nobody wants to turn nine or ten and not be baptized, I guess.

After I sit down, I turn around to look back at my grandmother and mother. They look proud and are smiling, and my mother is wiping her eyes with her handkerchief. They sure look different from how they looked when the chicken burned up. I turn back and I start thinking about my daddy. I wish he was here. I wish I could turn around and he would be sitting back there with Mother and Sweetmama. I wonder whether he would think I was doing the right thing doing this, knowing everything that's happened to me.

When the revival meeting is over, everybody hug and kiss and say "God bless" and "Praise the Lord." We go down in the basement for the pot-luck supper. Miss Beulah Johnson takes a bite of Mother's coconut cake with the pineapple-lemon filling and says, "Sure is good. I like that smoky taste."

10

AMY FROELICH'S DRESS

Everybody is excited at my house but me. Mother is sitting in the kitchen every night making a long white robe and a scarf to tie up my head.

Sweetmama is embroidering my name in white on my robe. "Maybe you save it, give it to your little girl to wear when she's eight years old, ready to be baptized."

"How come she got to be eight? Can't she be twelve?" I ask.

"She can be any age. Just in a family like ours we want everybody be part of the church young as they can start looking at life serious, choosing the right over the wrong."

She puts down her embroidery and lights a Lucky Strike. She stopped rolling her own when Yoki's got in more cigarettes. "These bad for me, I know," she says again, "but one ain't going to hurt."

"Thought you going to give them up," says Mother, trying not to frown. She always used to say before Sweetmama come, "Nothing but a chimney should smoke or a bar-be-que pit." But she's never said it all the time my grandmother's been here because she doesn't want to make Sweetmama feel bad. I know that's what she's thinking, though.

Mother looks over at me threading her needle for her and she smiles and says, "You going to try to keep out of trouble, puddin'? See it coming and step aside? Girl your age, if you keep on doing what you do, by the time you grown, burden be too heavy." She laughs.

But I don't think it's funny. I bet she wouldn't be laughing if she knew what Chuckie and I did.

After supper when Mother and Sweetmama are washing the dishes in the kitchen, I go into the other room and take the pink dress out of the chifforobe. I hold it up to me and look into the vanity mirror and make a face. I sit down on the vanity stool and look in the back of the neck, and there is a little white tag. I knew it would be there. All of my clothes have those tags, and they usually say "A. Froelich" or "Amy" or "Amy Froelich." I got a lot of Amy Froelich's clothes.

When Sweetmama goes rummaging, she *looks* for Amy
Froelich's clothes for me.

"Well," Mother always says to Sweetmama, "Amy however-you-say-her-last-name deserves a thank-you from us. It's one lucky thing for us her mother gives her things to St. Matthew's."

It's not my luck. I put that old pink dress back into the chifforobe and take out the catalog and sit on Mother's bed with the dusty rose chenille bedspread on it. I turn to the page where the navy-blue-and-white spring outfits are. There is a girl who is first just wearing the princess-style dress with the white collar and cuffs, and then she has on the whole outfit with the coat and the white gloves. She is about my age. She has yellow hair and pink lips that are smiling. I wonder whether Amy Froelich looks like that.

One time I brought some library books home. In one of the books I found a long yellow strand of hair. Some little girl, maybe Amy Froelich, had leaned over the book, and her hair had dropped on the page. She probably didn't see it happen, or maybe she left it there on purpose so the next reader could find it and could see that Amy had read the book too.

I took down one of my braids and got Mother's sewing scissors, and when nobody was looking, I cut a strand of my hair all curly-kinky and placed it in the crease of the book along with that yellow strand of Amy Froelich's hair.

I wondered who would find them and what they would

think of the two strands of hair. Maybe they would think that this little black girl and this little white girl were friends and were reading the book together. But that's not possible here in Missouri now in 1943. Someday, my teacher Mrs. Long tells us, we will all be as one, but that time is not here yet.

I take out the catalog again and I am looking at Amy Froelich's picture in her navy-blue Easter outfit. I wonder why Sweetmama never found an outfit like that at the rummage. I'm sure Amy had one. Maybe she likes it so much, she won't let her mother give it away.

Mother comes in and sits down beside me.

"Bobby, you really want that outfit, don't you?"

I nod yes, and those big tears pop into my eyes again. Mother can make me cry when her voice sounds all soft like that. I just want to climb on her lap and lay my head against her chest. But I'm trying not to act like such a baby.

"I guess there's time to order that outfit for you," she says, pulling me into her arms.

"You mean it?" I ask, but I know she does. She's got a big smile on her face.

"You going to be baptized this Easter, and I guess you're entitled to something new."

I keep giving her big kisses all over her face until she says, "Stop that, you squeezing my neck to death."

The next day at school I feel good because I can say to Shirley and Audrey that I'm ordering, too, and be telling the truth.

"I don't believe it," says Audrey.

"You better believe it."

"You ain't never got nothing new and ain't no reason to get something this Easter," says Audrey.

I can't help it. I try not to do something bad but I get so mad with that Audrey that I just walk right past her and slam my foot on top of hers, hard.

She screams, and the teacher looks up and sees Audrey's mouth still open and sends her to see the principal. Shirley just looks at me and presses her lips together to keep from laughing. I just love Shirley. I go over to the reading area and pick up the B encyclopedia. Mrs. Long loves me. I hear her tell the principal that if nobody else in this room goes to college, she bets I will. She's right. I have been reading the encyclopedia to find out everything I need to know about life. Mrs. Long excuses me from handwriting practice so that I can do the encyclopedia. She says I need the challenge.

When Audrey comes back from the principal's office with red eyes, I decide to make her even madder. What she hates the most and everybody else can't stand either is when Mrs. Long sits with me and me alone and plays chess. "Ain't never heard of no chess," some of them say, looking at the board like it's something strange going to bite them.

I was reading about chess in one of my library books and I told Mrs. Long I wanted to learn how to play, and she bought a set with little white and black pieces and a book telling how the game is played. She sits with me very serious after lunch, holding the book in one hand and mumbling over the pieces. "Might as well learn along with you," she says.

She's like that. She'll do something special with you if you ask her. In the summer she's always wiping drops of sweat off the tip of her nose with a white handkerchief, she's running around the room so much, doing this, doing that. All day the children call, "Mrs. Long, Mrs. Long . . ." And one day it is very hot and she is holding her handkerchief to her forehead and bending over one girl's desk when somebody else calls. "Oh, stop calling my name!" she screamed real loud.

That was the first time she ever raised her voice, and the class got quiet and surprised. She walked back to her desk and sat down and put her head in her hands. "I'm sorry, children. I am very sorry."

We all got up and crowded around and took turns patting her on the back. We all love Mrs. Long. She's different from a lot of teachers, act like they glad to send their children outside to freeze in the winter for recess.

As Mrs. Long is placing the pieces on the chessboard, I wish I could tell her my problem. She's so smart, she could probably tell me the right thing to do about Yoki. But I can't tell her. I haven't even told my mother.

She looks up at me looking at her and she smiles. "Pay attention. We are going to learn about the knight's job," she says. All the time Audrey sitting at her desk, hiccuping, looking like she's a motherless child. Serves her right for being so nasty. Even so, I can't help but feeling a little bit bad about what I did.

I skip off the streetcar after school and run across the street and do a few turn-arounds, I'm so happy about getting a new Easter outfit like Shirley's and Audrey's. I feel so good, I almost pass by Yoki's, but my feet don't forget and they just turn me right back around and we go into the store.

Roger is talking to Mr. Okone, who works at the rope factory. My heart gives a lurch when I hear what they are talking about.

"I was wondering what he was doing deliverin' down by the river," says Mr. Okone. "Never thought it wasn't Mr. Strausburger down there so early in the morning."

"You mean to tell me you saw my horse and wagon a coupla months ago and never said nothing to me?" asks Roger, getting red in the face. "I've been screaming about this thing all over the place!"

"I been poorly. My leg's been actin' up," says Mr. Okone, who starts to lift his pant leg to show Roger.

"Never mind, never mind," says Roger, who looks like he's going to get sick if he has to look at Mr. Okone's poorly leg. I never thought a mean old cucumber like him would have a weak stomach. "Okay, okay," he says. "That's all water under the bridge. What else can you tell me about my wagon and horse?"

"Hi, Roger," I say, hoping I will drown out anything old Mr. Okone might say or maybe make him forget what he was about to say.

"Don't bother me now. Can't you see something important is happening here?" screeches that Roger.

"But I just want to say hi," I say, giving him my smile, which he must think is just as terrible as I think his laugh is.

"If you can't keep quiet, scram!"

I just stand there and pretend to be looking in the pickle barrel. Roger is too busy trying to find out what Mr. Okone saw that night to notice me.

"Did you see the driver?"

"It was bright 'cause of the snow, and the moon was full out. First I thought it was your uncle, but I couldn't see inside the wagon so good because I didn't have my seeing eyeglasses on. Then I heard her say 'Giddap.'"

"Her?" Roger looks surprised. "Are you sure you heard right?"

"I'm sure. I may not see so good but I can still hear perfect!" says Mr. Okone.

"Okay, okay, I believe you," says Roger, squinching up his eyes as if that was going to give him better brains.

"How was it that you were down that way, Mr. Okone?" I ask in my sweet voice.

"Well, littleun, I was on the night shift at the rope factory not too far away, and I just was going down by Mrs. Clay's shack to check on it. I promised her I'd look over her old house once in a while. Not for no particular reason 'cept she sure did love that place."

"Okay, okay, let's get back to the horse," says :117
Roger, cutting in. "Can you think of anything else?"

"There was something else," Mr. Okone says, rubbing his chin, "but I can't remember right now. It'll come to me. These things always do, but can't rush them . . ."

I am holding my breath. I start to pray he won't remember whatever it was. Roger cuts him off just in time.

"I don't have time to talk anymore, Okone. I'll get your coal oil from the back."

When Roger goes into the back, I smile my real smile at Mr. Okone and start toward the door. "I'll be seeing you, Mr. Okone."

"So long, youngun."

I get out of there fast and almost knock down Mr. Jenkins, who is carrying a big sack of flour to his shop.

"I'm sorry, Mr. Jenkins."

"Umph, don't worry about it, Bob. It's an accident. Where you going in such a hurry? To a fire?"

"Worse than that. Much worse than that, Mr. Jenkins," I say, taking off again.

I run all the way home and into the hall and knock hard on Mrs. Beene's door. When she opens it, she looks down at me like she's ready to say, "How come you knockin' loud to wake the dead?"

"Mrs. Beene, somebody saw you!" I say, out of breath.

She shoves me inside quick, and we go into the kitchen.

"Mr. Okone was in the grocery store a minute ago and he was telling Roger that he saw somebody driving away with Yoki."

"That ain't nothin'."

"It is something, because Mr. Okone told Roger that he didn't see who it was because he doesn't see so good but that he heard a voice . . . he said *her* voice. That's you!"

"Don't worry."

"Mrs. Beene, you don't know Roger. When they invented mean, they invented Roger."

Mrs. Beene starts to smile when I say that.

"That's not funny, Mrs. Beene; it's the truth."

She looks serious again and gets up and starts to dry a few spoons on the sink and put them away.

"You go on home. Everything turn out all right."

Sweetmama fixes supper and leaves it warming on the stove. She puts on her coat and calls out to me, "Your mother will be home in a little bit. You two go on and eat. I'll be over at the church late, tryin' to get some packages off to the soldiers."

"Yes, ma'am," I call out from the other room. I am sitting at the vanity trying to think of a way to write my daddy about all my problems without making it sound like bad news. I just *have* to tell him what's going on.

So I write this:

How are you? I am still getting into trouble but what's new about that? (smile) I'm not supposed to write you any bad news but I've got a few things to tell you that are not so bad. In fact, they are funny, really funny. For one thing, I think you would have laughed and laughed when you heard that an old funny-looking horse named Yoki got rescued by two kids who didn't want him to be sent to the glue factory and that a really funny-looking lady helped them do it. You should have seen the funny looks on their faces when the kids went to feed the horse at the hideout the next day and (ha, ha) guess what? He was gone. I bet you're just laughing over that. And then the kids got real worried after the owner of the horse said whoever stole him would be put in jail. (smile). It just could make you laugh and laugh the way those kids worried. The lady who helped them said she would take all the blame if anybody ever found out. Isn't that a funny (ha, ha) thing to do?

Now somebody thinks he saw who took the horse from the hideout and I'm probably going to fall out laughing myself when they take this lady off to jail or the crazy house. There is one tiny part to this that's not so funny but maybe it'll make you smile a little: One of the kids is worried about getting baptized with this secret she's carrying around. I hope this part makes you laugh too and not worry.

Love, *Bob*

11

THE GIFT

:120   One day we come to school and Mrs. Long gives us
our spelling test and our arithmetic and then she stands
in front of the class and she is holding a record.

"Class, I have something very upsetting to tell you,"
she says, and there are tears in her eyes. "It is very,
very unfortunate," she says, taking her handkerchief
out of her sleeve.

"Last night I received word from Shirley's mother
that Shirley's father was killed in the war."

All the children are quiet. I wondered where Shirley
was when I came in. I just sit there. My head feels big

and tight like it's blown up, and it hurts over my eyes. I
feel like I need to pop my ears. I can't hear Mrs. Long
too well for a minute.

Mrs. Long wipes her eyes and then runs her handkerchief around the record. She runs it around and
around as she talks.

"Somebody tell me what respect we pay to a soldier
killed in the war when he dies fighting for his country?"

A boy stands up and says, "We can put our heads
down and place our hands over our hearts for a minute."

"We can stand up, that's right. And we can place our
hands over our hearts."

"Or we can salute like I see in the movies," says
Audrey.

"We can do that too."

She goes over to the record player and puts on the
record. "I have a record here with taps on it. It's special
music that is played for a soldier who dies. Now, while
this is playing, you think about Shirley and her father
and all the soldiers fighting in the war."

It is slow, sad horn music: dum da dumm, dum da
dumm, dum da dumm. And when it's finished, we all sit
back down. I don't think about a thing when the music
is playing. I just stand there. When I sit down, I hear
something drop on my copy paper. I feel so bad, my
tears falling like rain.

If Shirley's father, Leon, is dead, then maybe my
daddy is next. Ever since I saw what happened to men
fighting in the war in *Life* magazine, I imagine that my
father is riding in a jeep and it rolls over and some-

thing blows up, or he is just going somewhere to get dinner or is out shopping or something and somebody come up quick behind him and then he's hanging over a fence like wet clothes. Now Shirley's father, Leon, is killed. It's the first time I ever knew anybody whose father was killed in the war. There's no reason my daddy can't get killed too.

We go over to see Shirley and her mother after my mother gets off from work. As we come up the front walk, I can see that somebody has sewn a gold star over the blue star in the window. I start to cry when I see it, and Mother and Grandmother stand outside with me until I can stop. "You got to help Shirley feel better. Ain't going to work you walk in cryin'," says Mother.

When we go in, somebody standing behind Shirley's mother's chair and running fingers through her hair to stop her from crying. She looks up when she sees me standing by the door and says in this wavery voice, "Shirley in the other room, sugar. Go on in. She be glad to see you."

My mother gives me a little push, I'm moving so slow. I can't help it. Shirley's in there with no daddy coming home. That makes me scared.

I stick my head in the door real shy and I see Shirley sitting up on the bed, staring off like she does sometimes. I wonder if she's imagining she's seeing her father killed or what.

"Shirley," I say.

She turns around. "Daddy got killed," she tells me.

"Ain't no use to listening to no baseball games."

"We can still listen. Ain't nothing wrong with that," I tell her, taking little tiny steps over to the bed.

"You been crying?" I ask, trying to look close into her face. It's getting dark, and I don't know whether I'm supposed to turn on the light. I don't know whether I'm supposed to talk in a normal voice or whisper, things so different.

She doesn't answer me, just stretches out on the bed and turns her head away. I stretch out on the bed too, with my scarf and coat still on. I put my arm around her shoulders. In the dark I keep thinking maybe Shirley's father, Leon, he can see me taking care of his child. We still the terrible twins, I want to tell him. Don't worry; Bob and Shirley, they'll be friends no matter what. Only how do you tell him something like that? Do you whisper it in the dark or in the light?

At home everybody is quiet at supper. Mother holds my hand under the table and talks real soft to me. "You try to eat, Bob. Not eating ain't going to bring Leon back. You feel better you remember him sittin' around this very table laughing and joking and eating," she says, but that just makes tears come to her eyes.

"What we got to do is pray he didn't suffer; he go easy," says my grandmother.

"We going to write Daddy about it?" I ask.

"Don't know right now. Maybe it's better we wait till he gets home," Mother says.

* * *

Two weeks from Easter Sunday Mother and my grandmother go to the funeral. They wouldn't let me go.

"You been pokin' around, not eatin'," says Mother. "That funeral everybody cryin' and carryin' on, be too much for you."

"But I want to be with Shirley," I say.

"We'll go sit with the family after the funeral at the supper. It'll be better you see her there."

I stay with Mrs. Beene until the funeral is over and they come to take me to Shirley's. I help Shirley a lot at the supper. She keeps dropping things like peas on her white dress and spilling grape juice on her white socks and shoes and I keep cleaning it up. When she starts to cry, I take my handkerchief and wipe her face.

After we eat, she lays across the bed to rest. I take down her two long braids her mother tied with white ribbons and put white paper flowers in and brush her hair real slow, like my mother does for me sometimes, until she goes to sleep. Just before she closes her eyes, she says to me, "Thanks for helping me." I feel better after she says that. That's what a friend can do for you.

I come home from school the next day, and a big brown box is sitting on the kitchen table. I open it before I take off my coat. The dress, the coat with the removable white collar and cuffs, the white gloves and two pairs of ankle socks, one pink and one white, are all there. Everything *smell* so new. I can't talk I am so

excited. I take the box in the other room and change
into my never-worn outfit.

"You do look good," my grandmother says, standing in the doorway, and then she looks at it with a keen eye. "Needs pressing, and that hem don't look too straight to me."

But I don't care. I keep staring at myself in the mirror. I can't believe it. I can't believe it. I feel as if I'm going to tip over.

"Take them off. You be wearing them out before your mother have a chance to see you in them," Sweetmama calls from the kitchen.

I go into the kitchen, and my grandmother is cutting up apples for a pie. "I'm scared to get up and get baptized in front of all those people, Sweetmama."

"Everything'll turn out fine. Baptizing a good feeling. You step foot in the church next Sunday, you smell the lilies and the other flowers, you see the people all dressed up and happy. Easter the time when everything comes up new. It's a new chance for everybody. You remember your baptism, everything about it, all your life. When I was young down in the country, we got baptized off the riverbank just like Jesus did with his friend John the Baptist. They still do to this day.

"I remember they be a hundred people all dressed in white—men, women, and children. Early on Easter Sunday morning just when the sun begin to rise. All the friends and family stand on the shore and sing. Some come out of the water shouting, 'I'm saved, I'm saved.' They raise they arms above they head and look up, like a light shining down on them that hurt they eyes. But we lookin' on can't see nothin' but how dark it still is that early in the mornin'."

I go over and sit on my grandmother's lap. There is nothing feels so good like this.

"After that everybody dry off, go back to the church and then go out to the park and have one big meal. It be warm by then. I'm telling you," she says, lighting a Lucky Strike, "everybody bringing something good from home. They would have forty different kinds of sweet-potato pies, one more fancy than the next. Everybody trying to outdo everybody else, because there is no celebration as big as the one we have when you get baptized."

Maybe if there was a hundred people with me, I wouldn't feel so scared. Or maybe if we got baptized in a river instead of a pool in the church, it would seem more natural, and I think I could do it. There is the river Niger in Africa that Mrs. Long is teaching us about. The people there up and down that river do everything around it. They fish, they wash clothes, everything. But where we get baptized is a pool that used to be under the choir stand before we built a new church, and the choir always had to move when somebody was baptized.

But now we got this new church and the pool is sitting in front of the altar on top of the floor with high glass sides. It looks like a big square goldfish bowl. There is a stuffed white bird hanging from a string over

it, and when the water is in it, little waves flap against :127
the sides. You can see the person being baptized walk
down the steps into the water. The water looks heavy
and green, and it pushes up the white robe so you can
see their legs. Then Reverend Hovis, he comes and puts
his big hand over the person's nose and pushes them
down under the water. I always hold my breath at this
part. Suppose they slip and really fall all the way under.
Suppose I slip. Suppose Reverend Hovis have a heart
attack and let go of me.

One week to go. At school I'm scared, at home I'm
scared. It's the last day of school before Easter-week
vacation starts. I ask Audrey if she is scared, and she
puts her nose in the air and says, "Of course not," like
she heard Bette Davis say in the movies. I ask Shirley
when we're eating lunch together and she says "Yes."

"Well," I say at recess when Shirley and Audrey and
me are jumping rope, "only one thing good about next
Sunday. We're going to look just like triplets in our
navy-blue outfits."

"I won't have one," Shirley says.

"Whatchoo mean?" I say. I'm really surprised.

"Mama, she forgot to order it after my daddy . . .
daddy died and . . . and . . ."

"Oh, that's bad," I say, patting Shirley's hand. She's
about to cry.

"Yeah, that's terrible," says Audrey, taking her other
hand.

"Shirley, don't cry," I say. "You cry, I cry too."

"Me too," says Audrey, who can be nice when she wants to be.

Mrs. Long is on duty in the yard, and she comes over and asks us what is wrong. We stop crying and just look at her with big eyes. She takes her handkerchief out of her pocket that smells like soap flakes and she wipes our faces with it.

We don't say a thing except "Thank you" in a little voice, and she looks at us about to say something, and then some old boy kicks a ball right into her legs. We have to run after him and catch him and bring him over to her. She walks away talking to him, and we put our arms around each other's shoulders and stand looking at the ground until the bell rings.

Ever since Monday our place has been a mess, and that's no way to spend a vacation. Everything's out of place, Mother and Sweetmama scrubbing, polishing, dusting so much getting ready for Easter Sunday.

"Got to turn out winter, welcome in spring," Sweetmama says.

Me, I don't feel like doing a thing. I'm just low. I can't help but think about Shirley with nothing new for Easter and no daddy, either.

I don't see Shirley again until I go to the Easter-program rehearsal at church. After that I feel even worse. I come home and I'm not hungry for supper. I take Rose and go to bed early.

"You sick or something?" asks Mother.

"No, ma'am," I say.

"Baby, something really wrong. What is it?" she asks, looking real close at me as I hold on tight to Rose, all curled up on the bed.

"Mother," I say, real quiet, "I don't want to go to no funeral for my daddy."

"Bob, we don't think about what might happen someday. We got to think about now. I don't want your daddy to die, either. I want him to be here to see my girl grow up. It be good if you forget about your troubles by helping somebody else. That way your heart not be so heavy."

Mother goes into the other room, and a little later I tell her I'm going to sit in the thinking chair in the hall bathroom for a while.

Maybe Mother is right. Maybe I haven't been doing enough for somebody else. The last time was for Yoki, and she is right, when I was having all that trouble, I didn't have time to worry about anything.

I hear Mrs. Walker's mother calling, "Lucille, Lucille," and I know Mrs. Walker is coming for the chair, so I quick get up and go back into my room.

"Mother," I say, coming into the other room holding on to Rose, "I want to do something for somebody else like you say, but I'm afraid you'll get mad at me for doing it."

"Now, why I get mad when you do something for somebody else?"

"Well, okay," I say, going over to the chifforobe. "I want to give Shirley my navy-blue-and-white Easter outfit."

"You got to be kiddin'," Mother says, rearing back like she wants to see me better.

"I'm not. Her mother forgot to order from the catalog after Shirley's father got killed, so she's not going to have an outfit like this for Easter Sunday."

"What you want to do shows a good thought and a big heart, and it shows how deep your friendship is, but you been wanting something new for a long time. Don't seem right you give it away."

"I want to do it," I say.

"Why don't you give her the pink dress. It's beautiful, and she don't have to know it comes from the rummage."

"She'll know it comes from there. She knows everything I wear comes from there. And even if she would like it, I want to give her what she really want to wear for Easter."

Mother looks at me for a long time. "I'm going to start supper. You put on the outfit again and you decide. Whatever you want to do, I go along with it."

I put on everything, including the new white ankle socks and my patent-leather shoes. I stand in front of the vanity and look at myself. I look so good. I love this navy-blue outfit. I take out the catalog and bring it over and put it down on the stool and turn to the girl in the same outfit who is probably Amy Froelich. I look at her and at me in the mirror. We look a lot alike except

we're different colors. There is one other difference.
She's smiling like she's happy, and I'm not happy. I
don't feel good at all, and I know I will feel just like
this when I wear the outfit on Sunday. But I know
Shirley will feel happy in it.

"Well, what you think?" asks Mother, standing in the
doorway.

"I want to give it to Shirley."

"Okay, then, you take it off and we'll give it to Shirley."

I come into the kitchen after I put the outfit back in
the box. "I guess I did teach you something about quality after all," she says, laughing a little bit. "It don't just
have to be in the material of the dress. It can be in the
heart too.

"Come on," she says, "let's finish packing it up. Tonight is Wednesday. Guess we better take it over after
supper."

"Shirley need something for her head," I say.

"That means you won't get no Easter hat with ribbons running down the back that you been telling me
you want."

"And no white gloves, either," I say, putting the
gloves in the box.

Mother and I go downtown and we pick out a white
straw hat for Shirley, and I beg her and beg her until
she buys a handkerchief with three cats embroidered in
the corner for Mrs. Beene.

We come back home and pack up everything.

Mother opens the icebox and looks at the coconut

cake she baked in the morning for Easter dinner. She used all the sugar she'd been saving for that cake.

"You going to give her that too?" I say.

"Why not?" says Mother, reaching for it.

"But . . ."

She puts her finger to her lips, and I stop, but that cake makes my mouth water and my stomach growl just looking at it.

"You ever hear of giving till it hurts?" she says, laughing.

"No, but I know what it feels like now," I tell her, crossing my eyes.

12

THE BARGAIN

I feel so good when I wake up. Mother just loves me for what I did for Shirley, and all yesterday evening Shirley kept patting my hand after she saw what I brought her, she was so happy.

I have a good day helping Sweetmama polish the furniture and hang out the wash. She helps me put on some of Mother's fingernail polish even though she doesn't like to see little girls with red, red fingernails. But then Chuckie comes over in the evening, and I forget all about being happy. I can't help it. When I see him I think of Yoki and then of Roger and Mr. Okone and what he knows, and then I think of Mrs. Beene, who's going to get caught. Being happy is just long gone.

"I know Mr. Okone is going to remember," I tell Chuckie as we sit talking real low on the front steps.

"I been thinking about that ever since you told me," says Chuckie.

"I got a thought that's been worrying me for days," I say.

"Oh, no, something else?"

"It's bad enough if they found out and Mrs. Beene had to go to jail. But I think if they know she did it, they're going to put her somewhere much worse than jail."

"Where you talking about?"

"In an insane asylum."

"You crazy."

"I'm not. What the police going to think when they start asking her questions and she doesn't answer them. They're going to think she's touched in the head like your mother thinks."

"They might put her in one of those places where they put you in a cell with mattresses around the walls, and if you complain, they tie you up in a white shirt so you can't move your arms," Chuckie says. "I saw that in a movie once."

"Where're you going?" Chuckie asks, nervous, as I start to walk to Yoki's Grocery.

"I just want to see if Roger knows any more about that-certain-person Mr. Okone saw driving the milk wagon."

"You better keep away from there," he says, walking
beside me. "Roger's going to start wondering about all
those times you come nosying in there."

"He's not smart enough to figure that out. He just
thinks I'm a pesty kid ain't got nothing better to do."

"I'll be seeing you around," says Chuckie, and he
takes off at a trot.

"You scared!" I scream after him. I don't know why,
but I feel like crying. I feel alone, like nobody cares
that I got to tell Roger the truth; not even Mrs. Beene.

Roger looks up from putting ration stamps in some
books when I come in.

"Come to check on that horse again?"

"Mr. Okone give you any more hints?"

"He's coming by tomorrow night to see my uncle,
play some checkers upstairs. I'll ask him then."

"Maybe he made a mistake that he heard a woman's
voice."

"Don't think so."

"If it was a woman, would you want the police to put
her in jail?"

"Why not?" he says, smiling. "A thief is a thief."

"I got to go, Roger," I say. "My mother says save
her some eggs. Got to have them to dye in a couple of
days."

I walk home slowly. One thing I know for sure.
There's no way I can stand to see Roger watching Mrs.
Beene be put in handcuffs and saying, "A thief is a
thief."

I go inside and knock on Mrs. Beene's door.

"I'm going to tell Roger the truth, Mrs. Beene," I say.

"When?" is all she says.

"Tomorrow. I just can't turn around and go back tonight. But I got to do it."

"No you don't."

I just look up at Mrs. Beene. I can't tell her that if Mr. Okone remembers, this time next week she might be in the crazy house. She's just looking down at me, expecting me to say something. Her eyes look like flashlights, and her lips look more locked up than ever, and the frown between her eyes is making a perfect V. For a minute she looks scary to me, but then it passes, and she is the same old Mrs. Beene, a friend of mine.

"Good night," I say, and turn and go up the stairs real slow.

I say good evening to my grandmother, who is cooking dinner, and I go into the other room and change into my nightgown.

"Oh, my. You sick or something this close to Easter?" asks Sweetmama when I come back into the kitchen.

"No, ma'am," I say, and begin to pull out the rollaway bed. "I'm just sleepy."

"Then go in and lay down on your mother's bed. I'm having some church ladies over tonight. We're knitting socks for the boys overseas. Won't be finished until late."

"Yes, ma'am."

Sweetmama comes in with some hot biscuits and some buttermilk. But I can't eat a thing.

She sits on the bed and puts her hand on my forehead. She has to squinch up her eyes because the smoke from her cigarette is curling up and stinging them.

"You don't feel hot."

"I'm not sick, Sweetmama, I'm just real tired. My head's so heavy, I just got to lay it down."

I wake up early the next morning. There is something I have to do today, and I'm going to do it after Good Friday services at the church. Time goes fast, because I'm afraid to do what I have to do. It seems like we just get to church when the service is over. Now it's time to turn myself in to Roger. Maybe the police will let me off long enough to have Easter Sunday and get baptized. That's one thing I want to do, because after I tell Roger I'll know for sure that I did the best I could with everything that's been bothering me. No doubt about it.

Sweetmama lets me go visit Chuckie after we eat lunch. "Good thing you going over there," she says, putting the chairs upside down on the table. "Got to mop and wax this floor. Don't want you tracking through." And then she laughs. "I'm starting to act like that friend of yours downstairs."

I hurry over to Chuckie's, and when he comes out on his porch, I whisper, "I'm going to tell Roger today."

"Why do you have to do that?" Chuckie asks, getting mad.

"Because Mr. Okone is going to be at Mr. Strausburger's tonight playing cards, and Roger's going to ask him if it's come to him yet what he saw."

"He might not remember anything."

"But he might."

"Why don't you wait and see?"

"Because if he does remember that it's Mrs. Beene, then it'll be too late."

"She'll still be in trouble if he remembers even after you've told Roger. She'll be in trouble no matter what. So why should you get us in trouble too?"

"If she gets in trouble, then I get in trouble too!"

"I don't understand you," says Chuckie. "I don't want to get in trouble just because somebody else is."

"Even if you *should* be in trouble because you're to blame?" I say.

Chuckie thinks about this and then he says, "Why do you have to be such a big mouth?"

"Why do you have to be such a baby?"

"Don't you call me that," he says and grabs me by one of my braids. It hurts. It really does, but I don't care. I sink my teeth into his arm. He screams and lets me go. He looks like he wants to knock my head off but he doesn't do it. If I go, he goes. We just stand there on his porch trying to stare each other down. I wish he'd never been thought of.

I start down the porch steps real fast. "I'm going to see Roger right now," I scream at him over my shoulder. I'm so mad. I don't know why I'm rushing like

that. All I'm doing is hurrying to get myself put in
jail.

I'm standing on the corner near his house waiting for an old car to go chug, chugging past when that old Chuckie comes up. I pretend I don't even see him.

"You're not really going to tell him, are you?"

I don't say a word. I just cross the street and head for Yoki's. I'm so mad at Chuckie, I *want* to get there fast because I *want* to see him put in jail, even if I go myself.

"Hey, wait for me," he says, running to catch up.

He tries to race me to the grocery just to be mean. "Whatchoo in such a hurry for?" I say. "You too scared to go in."

"I'm not scared. I just think you crazy to tell about something you did if nobody will ever find out."

"Maybe it looks crazy to you, but it's not crazy. It's the right thing to do."

He gets there first and starts to open the door. "You get outta my way," I say. I'm so mad, I feel like spitting.

"You think you're so big and bad, don't you," he says, sounding like he could spit too.

"Badder than you," I say.

"Ain't nobody badder than me," he says, bringing his face up so close to mine, I start to bite his nose.

"Hey, you two, cut out that fighting!"

We jump, we're so surprised to hear Roger's voice.

"Close that door and either come in or out but don't stand there fighting like two roosters."

I give Chuckie the worst look I can think of and step inside. He steps inside too.

"Well, what do the Bobbsey Twins want today?" asks that horrible Roger.

"We got something to tell you," says Chuckie before I can open my mouth. I look at him, surprised. I never thought he would say a word.

"Don't just stand by the door; come in."

"We can talk from here," Chuckie says, grabbing my hand. When he does that, my heart just turns over. That Chuckie—one minute I hate him, the next I just love him to death.

"What's the matter? Think I'll bite? Well, I won't. I just grind children up for hamburger. Want to come see?" he asks.

"We have something important to tell you," I say, holding Chuckie's hand tight.

"You said that."

"You're not going to like it," I say.

"Well, what is it?"

"We took Yoki," we say together.

"You what?"

"We took your horse," Chuckie says, backing us a little toward the door.

"You two? Who're you kidding?" he asks, laughing. "You couldn't steal a row of flowers without getting caught."

"We did take him," Chuckie says.

"Don't waste my time. What kind of joke is this, anyway?"

"It's no joke," I say. "We're telling the truth."

"Look," says Roger, coming from behind the counter, "I have had enough of your nosying around about that horse. I don't know what kind of game you're playing, but I want you out of here telling bald lies."

"We're not lying!" I say.

"You heard Okone yourself say that he heard a woman's voice telling the horse to get going."

"He didn't say a woman's voice," I say, getting hot. "He said he heard *her* voice. That voice was me!"

"And what did you do with him?" asks Roger, looking like he's caught us now.

"We hid him," says Chuckie.

"Where?"

"We can't tell you," I say.

"You're both full of baloney," he says, disgusted.

"We did take him," I say, getting even hotter. When I get this mad, watch out. "I'm glad we did too. Who do you think you are, killing a horse just because you feel like it!"

"All right, I have had enough of your lip, you bratty kid. Now, get out of this store before I—"

"You're not going to do nothin' to her!" says Chuckie.

"Oh, yeah. If she was mine, I'd whack the daylights out of her."

"You and what army!" says Chuckie, balling up his fist.

"You touch me, and my daddy will take care of you!" I say, moving back a little.

"Your father is over there in the Pacific trying not to be shot to pieces. He can't do a thing for you!"

That's it. I'm so mad, I can't see. Two big tears roll down my face, and before I know it I'm biting that ugly, dumb cucumber in the leg. I keep on biting him until he starts to scream. He raises his hand to hit me, but Chuckie slams him in the arm with his knapsack and then tackles him and knocks him down with me still holding on to his thigh with my teeth. We're scrambling around on the floor in the sawdust when we hear a lot of racket outside. It sounds like chickens cawing and cackling. I let go of Roger's leg, and Roger sits up.

"What's that?" he asks, rubbing his thigh where I almost took a plug out.

Chuckie and I run to the door and look out.

"Oh, no," says Chuckie as we rush outside.

"Mrs. Beene, go back!" I scream.

But Mrs. Beene is too busy parking a beat-up old pickup truck that's filled to the top with chickens. Feathers are flying all over the place, and the noise is so loud that Mr. and Mrs. Jenkins come out of their bakery to find out what's going on.

"Mrs. Beene," I say. "You shouldn't have come here."

Mrs. Beene ignores me and gets out of the truck. She walks around to the back of the pickup truck and takes a look at all those chickens going crazy. That's when I see Yoki's wagon hitched onto the back.

"Oh, no," whispers Chuckie. "Off to the crazy
house."

"Chuckie!"

Mrs. Beene walks up to Roger, who is standing in the doorway of the grocery store still rubbing his leg and acting like he can't believe his eyes. "I took your horse," she says.

It's the first time I ever heard her say anything to anybody except me and Chuckie.

"She didn't do it. She didn't," I scream. I just feel like crying.

Roger looks like he's going to start jumping up and down like Rumpelstiltskin he's so mad. "Now you say you took the horse, and she says she took the horse."

Mrs. Beene just points to the back of the truck.

"That's my wagon!" Roger screams.

"It's Mr. Strausburger's wagon. Not yours!" says Chuckie.

"I'm bringing it back," says Mrs. Beene.

Mr. Jenkins walks up and says, "What's going on here? The whole block is disturbed by all this racket." As he is talking, other people cross the street to watch what's going on. I hope my mother and grandmother are at home right now and not thinking about taking a walk on Culpepper Street.

"She stole my wagon," Roger says, pointing to Mrs. Beene.

"That's hard to believe," says Mrs. Jenkins.

"She borrowed it, that's all," says Chuckie.

"I want that horse back," says Roger to Mrs. Beene.

"He just wants him back so he can have him killed at the glue factory for thirty-five dollars," I say to Mr. Jenkins.

"You mean he'll make thirty-five dollars if Yoki is killed?" he asks.

"It's nobody's business what I want to do with my horse," says Roger. "I'm calling the police and having this woman arrested for stealing my horse and wagon," Roger says.

"But here is the wagon," says Mr. Jenkins. "If she stole it, why is she parking it in front of your store?"

"You don't know what you're talking about," Roger says real nasty to Mr. Jenkins. "Just stay out of it."

"Mrs. Beene and Bobby are my business, and so is Chuckie. They are good customers and good neighbors," Mrs. Jenkins says.

"Business schmizness, a thief is a thief."

"He wants thirty-five dollars," I say.

"I got chickens instead," says Mrs. Beene. Everybody else stops talking all at once, they're so surprised that she is talking.

"You can't just come here and steal my property and months later expect me to forget everything just because you've brought some chickens!" says Roger.

"Why not?" asks Mrs. Jenkins. "If all you want is the thirty-five dollars. Here is a load of chickens worth more than thirty-five dollars in profit."

"He doesn't really want the money, he wants to see

somebody put in jail—that's what he wants," I say.

"Quiet, kid," Roger says, coming at me again. "You've said enough!"

"Don't you talk to Barbara Ann that way," Mrs. Jenkins says, shaking her finger in Roger's face.

"What's going on down there?" We all look up as Mr. Strausburger leans out of his bedroom window. "It sounds like the Buddy Baer–Joe Louis fight all over again."

"Mrs. Beene brought some chickens worth more than what Roger was going to get to kill Yoki, and he won't take them," I say, and then I turn that terrible smile of mine on Roger, who looks as if he can't wait to get his hands on me.

"Chickens? How many chickens?" Mr. Strausburger asks.

"Just take a look, Mr. Strausburger, take a look," I say, running over to the back of the pickup with chickens stuffed in there all squawking and clucking and feathers flying.

"Not bad. Not a bad haul," says Mr. Strausburger. "And where is Yoki?"

"He's on Mrs. Beene's farm, doing fine," I say, sending up my sunbeam smile for him.

"Uncle, let me handle this," says Roger.

"You're not handling it, Roger, just contributing to the noise level down there," Mr. Strausburger says.

"Uncle..."

"You're taking care of Yoki, Mrs. Beene, that it?"

Mrs. Beene has done all the talking she's going to do today, and she just stares up at Mr. Strausburger.

"She sure is," I say, quick.

"Well, then, I want to thank you. I was too sick to make proper arrangements for my horse myself."

"Uncle!"

"Let me finish, Roger. I'm afraid I agreed to something that I probably couldn't have lived with once I got back on my feet. That horse meant a lot to me. We've waded through a lot of snowstorms, rainstorms, hailstorms, and heat waves, I'll tell you."

"But, Uncle, I—"

"Think, Roger, think, my boy. Where can we put all these precious chickens," said Mr. Strausburger. "They're a godsend during these hard times of rationing. Think, before Mrs. Beene changes her mind. I'll let her keep Yoki whether she gives us the chickens or not. I am so glad my horse is well and safe. I'm lucky she's not charging me for boarding him."

"But, Uncle, she's a thief. She stole him and didn't tell us. All these months I've been so worried about Yoki. The police have been looking . . . she can't get off like this. You're . . . you're even *thanking* her."

"That's right, I'm thanking her for saving Yoki. I find it hard to believe, Roger, that you were worried about Yoki's well-being."

"Just about whether he was going to get his thirty-five dollars!" says Chuckie, cutting his eyes at Roger.

"Roger, find it in your heart to wish Yoki a little peace and quiet and green grass," says Mr. Straus-

burger. "After all of those years of working, he deserves it."

"Would you like to be sent to be made into glue after you are too old to work in the store, Roger?" asks Chuckie.

I can't help it; I start to giggle. Chuckie was so serious when he said that. Roger gives me another one of those looks that say maybe he's going to put a hex on me.

"You could put the chickens in Yoki's old shed, Mr. Strausburger," I say, ignoring Roger.

"That's a good idea, Bobby. I'm going to ask you and Chuckie to tend them for me."

"We wouldn't mind doing that, Mr. Strausburger. We need to do something to show you we didn't mean to steal Yoki—just to keep him safe."

"Are you sure you're going to be able to part with them one after another as I need them?"

I think hard about that. I forgot how I can't stand to see animals killed and picked. And if I got to know them . . . "Well, I don't know," I say in a little voice. "I don't like to see anything killed."

"Then we'll think of something else for you to do," Mr. Strausburger says.

"I can tend the chickens by myself," says Chuckie. "Ain't nothing to it."

"A bargain," says Mr. Strausburger. "I'm satisfied, very satisfied. Roger, what about you? You've got your wagon back to sell, and Yoki is alive and, I'm sure, happy out there on the farm."

"Come on, Roger, lighten up," says Mr. Jenkins. "You've lucked into a sweet deal. I wish I had one like it. Me, I've got to depend on the black market for any extras."

Roger starts to say something and he just can't make himself do it. He gives me one more dirty look, and I just give him my twenty-six-tooth smile, which makes him turn red in the face. He just turns and stomps back into the store.

"You'll have to excuse my nephew," says Mr. Strausburger. "His manners have been lost somewhere along the way."

Mrs. Beene doesn't hear him because she is over at the truck. Now she's opening the gate and pulling out the first big box of noisy chickens. The Jenkinses go over to help her, and they start unloading those chickens. Chuckie and me, we just look at each other, and then I look up at Mr. Strausburger, who is leaning out the window watching them.

"Mr. Strausburger, when are you coming back to the store?" I ask.

"Soon, Bobby, soon. Seeing all those chickens go into the yard is making me feel better by the minute," he says, rubbing his hands together.

After the chickens are put in the shed and Mrs. Beene heads back to her farm to return her son's truck, Chuckie and I walk home and sit on the front steps for a minute, because it's warming up outside.

I hate to bring it up, but I have to.

"I got to tell my mother."

"Then she'll tell my mother."

"I can't help that."

"You can help it. You don't want to help it. You like trouble. You like it!"

"I don't like it. You wrong about that."

"Then why do you have to tell your mother?"

"Because everybody else knows but her. You wouldn't like it if Mr. Strausburger told your mother about it and you've been going around saying nothing, would you?"

"I guess you're right. She hates it if she hears something about me from somebody else before she hears it from me."

"My mother too. Well, get ready to have the punishment that's worse than any punishment you've ever gotten," I say, giving a groan.

"I might get a whipping on top of it," says Chuckie, looking worried.

"I don't care if I do. I'm so glad Mrs. Beene is not going to the crazy house. Think—is a whipping as bad as being in reform school?"

"I guess it ain't."

"That's where we could be instead of here."

We talk a little bit more. Then we know it's time to go and tell our mothers. Chuckie jams his hands in his pockets and starts to trudge off real slow.

He look so sad, I feel bad for him. I get up and walk over and look down at the tulips just coming up in the yard. I say to Chuckie, "Come look at that."

When he bends over and tries to see what I'm pointing at, I quick give him a kiss on the cheek. He pulls away like he just got a burn.

"Whatchoo do that for?" he says, rubbing his cheek and looking disgusted.

"You a friend of mine. Friends kiss," I say.

"No they don't," he says, looking around like he's afraid somebody saw us.

"Yes they do," I tease him.

"I'll be seeing you," he says. He looks like he's afraid to stay with me and he's afraid to go home and tell his mother how he stole Yoki. I just laugh, he looks so funny, like he's trapped, don't know what to do. But I stop soon's he's gone because I've got to do the same thing. This is going to be harder than telling Roger we stole Yoki. My mother is my heart and I'm her heart, but she is nobody to mess with when she's mad.

13

BOB FACES THE MUSIC

Sweetmama and Mother are sitting at the kitchen table looking like they've been waiting for me. This is not good.

"You get your business taken care of?" Sweetmama says.

"What . . . what business?" I ask, surprised. She can't mean about Yoki. She doesn't know about Yoki.

"You know what business," says Mother. "Down at the store."

They do know! I don't know how, but they do. I never expected this. I just stand there looking at them, trying to tell whether they are mad or what.

Mother's got her lips clamped together, and that's bad. Sweetmama is puffing real fast on her cigarette, like she's nervous, waiting for something she knows is going to happen to happen. I just walk over to the step and sit down and wait for the worst.

"Well?" asks Mother.

"Say something, young lady," says Sweetmama.

They just sit there looking at me. I can't help it; I just start to cry. It's been too much. Me thinking I'm going to jail, and then that Roger talking about my father being shot up with guns, and Chuckie pulling my braids; now my grandmother and mother looking at me like I'm a motherless child.

"Whatchoo crying about?" asks Mother. "I'm the one should be crying. I'm the only one in St. Louis don't know you been out in the middle of the night on the street in a snowstorm in a wagon you could have got yourself killed in."

"I'm sorry . . . I'm sorry," I say, and start crying all over again.

"Ummmph, ummmph, ummmph," says Sweetmama, shaking her head.

"Why you didn't tell me what was going on?" Mother asks, and she really looks like her feelings are hurt, which makes me cry even more.

"I couldn't tell you. Mrs. Beene would have been put in a crazy house!"

"Whatchoo talking about?" asks Mother.

"Mrs. Beene wanted to take the blame no matter what I said, and if they found out, she would go to the crazy farm because she acts so strange."

"That old crazy woman belongs in the crazy house," says Sweetmama. "She's the one stop by here with all them chickens and told us what was going on. First time I ever heard her talk. You can believe me, your mother and I told her just where she should go from now on, leading you in that kind of mischief. She ain't responsible."

"She's my friend, and all she did was help."

"Help!" says Mother. "You ever thought you could have been killed on that icy street, with cars skidding all over the place?"

"No, ma'am."

"Me, I wouldn't know a thing, just think you over there being a good citizen helping Chuckie wrap newspapers. I wouldn't even know you drowned in the river."

"I didn't drown," I say, shivering a little.

"Why didn't you tell us what you were studying on doing with that Chuckie?" asks Sweetmama.

"Because if I had told you, you wouldn't have let me do it."

"You right about that!" says Sweetmama.

"But we couldn't see Yoki killed!"

"Listen to me, young lady. You just a little girl. Even if it's something supposed to be a good deed, you are supposed to come and tell me about it. That's what

I'm here for. I'm your mother. This is your grandmother. What you think we here for? Just to wash clothes, cook the dinner?"

"No, ma'am," I say. I'm so tired, I wish they would tell me what my punishment is and get it over with.

"I got a good mind to pack up your clothes and send you down South with Sweetmama so you can stay out of trouble."

"You wouldn't!" I say, getting scared.

"That, or you got to start to realize that you were too young to take it on yourself to save that horse."

"If I'm too young to do that then maybe I'm too young to get baptized."

"Now, why you say that?" asks Mother.

"I'm supposed to put aside my childish ways and start to grow up. That's what Sweetmama says."

"What you did was childish, missy, you better believe it," says Sweetmama.

"It was not childish!" I say. "I did something to help Yoki, because it was wrong to kill him just because he was a bother to Roger."

"It wasn't childish to want to do that, but it wasn't too smart to go out there in a snowstorm and do it," says Mother.

"Sweetmama told me to do the best I could in life. Well, that was the best I could do."

They just sit there looking at me like they forgot how to talk. So I just keep on going. "The worst thing that I did was think about letting Mrs. Beene take the blame because I was scared of going to reform school."

"Who said you were going to reform school?" asks Mother.

"Roger did . . . well, he said whoever took Yoki would be put under the jail. I just didn't want to go to reform school. I was just scared. But it wasn't right to let Mrs. Beene take the blame. We took that horse. She just helped us out because she said we didn't know what we were doing."

"You been thinking all this time you going to jail?"

"Yes, ma'am."

"Then how come you told Roger after all?"

"Because Mr. Okone saw her taking Yoki from down by the river only he didn't really see her, he heard her voice because he don't see too well and he was going to remember something else he saw and tell Roger. I just couldn't let Mrs. Beene be put in the crazy house all because of Chuckie and me."

"You mean when you told Roger, you thought you would be going to reform school and you still did it?" Mother asks.

"Yes, ma'am."

They just sit there looking at me some more.

"I don't know what to say," says Mother. The good thing is she doesn't look so mad anymore. She's looking at me like she's surprised at what she's seeing. I want to go over and sit on her lap; tell her about Roger and Chuckie fighting with me, but I don't try it. I'm still in a lot of trouble.

I wonder what my daddy would say if he was here. Maybe he would be mad as Mother. That I couldn't stand; I just couldn't. He never gets mad at me. I wouldn't be used to it. I'd be so hurt, it would probably stop me from growing.

"Bob, are you sorry about what you did?" asks Mother.

"No, ma'am," I say. I know it's the wrong thing to say, but it's the truth.

Mother is surprised. "Whatchoo say?"

"I can't help it. I'm not sorry I saved Yoki's life."

"I mean you sorry you went off doing this thing without telling me what you were going to do?"

"I'm sorry I couldn't tell you and I'll never do anything like that again," I say.

"But you're not sorry you didn't tell me about this mess?"

I just look at her without saying anything. I just can't tell her I'm sorry when I'm not.

"Sorry, not sorry, don't mean a thing now," Sweetmama says. "The main thing here is that missy shouldn't have gone off and did what she did. She was supposed to go wrap newspapers, not do another thing; not even go to the store for an ice-cream cone, because that's not what we told her she could do. Now the problem is what we going to do about her not obeying the rules of this house."

"That's right," says Mother, looking angry all over again. Why can't my grandmother just be quiet. Here she is sticking her two cents in, nobody asks her.

"Do you understand why we upset?" asks Mother.
"That's important that you understand."

"I understand," I say.

"Then you'll understand why you getting punished," says Mother.

"Yes."

"Good. Because this year your Decoration Day, your Labor Day, your Fourth of July, and your Halloween belong to me."

That's the worst thing I ever heard of. "Mother," I say, starting to cry, "that's too much!"

"Nope. Like Goldilocks say, it's just right."

"But I won't be able to go to the church picnic on Decoration Day and I won't be going to the carnival on the Fourth of July and the fishing trip with Sweetmama on Labor Day . . . and . . . and . . . I can't go out trick-or-treating on Halloween!"

"That's what it means, honey," says Mother, and she really looks like she feels bad for me. "That way you be reminded of why you shouldn't have done what you did for almost six months."

"But you don't have to mess up all my holidays for me," I say. "I'm never going to do that again."

"That and anything else like it. Next thing I know, you be planning a trip to see that horse without telling anybody."

How did she know that? I *was* thinking about how I could get out to Vidalia to visit Yoki without anybody knowing. I don't understand how my mother can read my mind sometimes.

Then Mother comes over and sits down beside me on the step. I'm so low, I just keep my head hanging down, staring at those teacups painted on the linoleum. She takes my hand and says, "You a good person, Bob. I don't want you to think I'm punishing you for that.

"What you did for Yoki, maybe you should get a medal or a ribbon or something, and taking the responsibility for it even though you were scared to death, that shows me what kind of person you going to be—a leader. You make up your own mind and you do the right thing in the end. I'm proud of you, real proud. But we got rules around here, and they good rules too. They to make sure you grow up right. That's why you got the punishment, and I'm just as sorry about it as you."

"She just like her father for the world," says Sweet-mama, who is setting the table for supper. "She look just like you, Saree, but she act like him. Down in the country growing up, he always draggin' those animals home, fixing them up . . . couldn't never eat no 'possum, 'cause it been kilt and skinned . . . and always taking a lot on hisself.

"And gettin' in trouble, he wrote the book. Looks like you read it from cover to cover, missy. Always, like you, he was trying to do what was right . . ."

"And it come out wrong!" I say, feeling better.

"That's what he said, anyway."

"You really mean it? You think I'm just like my daddy?"

"For the world. People like you and him always

jumping up doing the right thing, being the hero. You
the kind of people worry a mother to death. You don't
hold back. He tried to save a friend of his from drown-
ing when he was nine and almost drowned hisself. I like
to have a heart attack," she says, sitting down at the
table and talking in a real soft voice. "I know he's off in
that war doin' the same thing. Being the hero."

Sweetmama brushes her eyes like she's crying, and
then she lights up a cigarette.

"Ain't nothin' wrong with that, Sweetmama. The
newspapers say people always giving parades and
speeches for soldiers come back a hero. I be proud my
daddy a hero."

"I don't care about his being a hero, I just want him
to come back here."

"Well, no need to keep on talkin' about what's happening in that war," says Mother, stirring the pot of
butter beans on the stove. "Don't help nothin', just
make this house a sad and waiting house. Ain't going
to be like that."

I'm tired. I go to bed soon as I eat. Mother and
Sweetmama sittin' on the bed holding my hands.
They're telling stories about all the trouble I've gotten
in since I was able to walk. They're laughing and giving
me kisses and laughing some more. "I could write a
book about this child," says Sweetmama. "Remember
when she was three. . . ." That's all I hear. I just go off
to sleep holding their hands tight.

14

EASTER SUNDAY

I'm sitting at the kitchen table reading a good book when Mother says, "Bob, we're going down to the ten-cent store before it closes. You get everything ready for your bath. I want you in bed early so you be in good shape for Easter Sunday."

"Yes, ma'am," I say.

When I finish my book I get everything out for my bath so Mother won't have anything to do but get the tub down and boil the water. Then I see the bowl of eggs on the table ready for dyeing. I'll do those, too, so everything will be done when they get home.

I get out the powder for the dyes and make the colors with water and vinegar. I love the smell of dyeing
the eggs. I take the little wire that's got a circle on one
end and dip the eggs. Some I let sit a long time, and
they turn deep pink and dark blue and green. My favorite color this year is yellow. I make four different-
color yellow ones. Once you get started, it's hard to
stop, and I wish we had more eggs.

Then I put the eggs on newspaper to dry. Next I'm
going to lick the tattoos and put them on. Not too
many. I don't like for the eggs to look like they got
scribble, scrabble on them.

When Mother and Sweetmama come back, I have
finished and cleaned up the cups I used to dye the eggs.

"You sure do a good job," says Mother, admiring
the eggs. "You cook them just right. Ain't none of the
shells cracked."

"I didn't cook them. They already cooked," I say,
my heart fluttering.

"You mean you dyed all these eggs raw?"

I just stand there with big eyes. "I didn't know they
needed cooking," I say.

Mother and Sweetmama start to laugh. They sit
down and laugh. They hold their sides and laugh like
it's hurting them. I don't think it's funny. Now I don't
have any Easter eggs to peel and eat tomorrow.

"Well, I tell you," says Mother, "sometimes the
things you do work out all right. Now, I still got a dozen
eggs, so hard to come by anyway, to cook."

I just go over and slump down on the top step and fold my arms and poke out my lip. But that just makes them laugh some more.

It's Easter Sunday!

Mother has stacked the eggs in a basket very carefully and put them in the center of the table. As for me, my Easter basket just have some of those old hard marshmallow eggs with the sweet, sweet candy covering which I hate.

I'm sitting on the side of the stove on a high stool while mother curls my hair into big fat Shirley Temple curls with the curling iron. I only get curls on Easter. Other than that, it's two braids stuck behind my ears.

"Don't know how come I'm doin' all of this work for it to be washed out," Mother says.

My grandmother is all ready. Her hat has big flowers all around it and a veil that touches her nose. She's smoking a cigarette because she can't when she is in church. "These Lucky Strikes seem stronger than usual," she says, looking down at the cigarette like something is wrong with it. "Don't know why I like them so."

She puts the cigarette out in the ashtray and goes over to look in the mirror over the sink. She's looking to see if her gray hair shows around the edges. She's got a black crayon she rubs around the edges makes her hair black again.

Mother finishes my hair, and I go into the other room and put on Amy's pink dress. It's all starched, and the skirt sticks out from my body like a bell.

Mother ties a pink ribbon with long streams to a comb and puts it in the back of my hair. "You look pretty, my puddin'," she says as she stands behind me looking in the vanity mirror. She leaves to finish dressing, and I sit on the vanity stool waiting for her. This is the day. I think about getting in that pool, but it don't seem real. One minute I feel hot and the next cold and then I'm all right again. I recite my Easter verse soft to myself in the mirror:

"And, behold, there was a great earthquake; for the angel of the Lord descended from heaven, and came and rolled back the stone from the door and sat upon it.

"His countenance was like lightning and His raiment white as snow. And for fear of Him the keepers did shake, and became as dead men. And the angel answered and said unto the women, Fear not ye: for I know that ye seek Jesus, which was crucified. He is not here; for He is risen, as He said. Come, see the place where the Lord lay and go quickly and tell His disciples that He is risen from the dead."

Mother said yesterday, "You sure did learn that verse fast after all. A whole month where you can't even remember how it started."

She's right. But it comes easy now that that's all I have to worry about.

I'm proud that my verse is so long. Every Easter Sunday after the baptizing, the Sunday school puts on a program. We have to get up on the stage; the boys bow and the girls curtsy. The older you are, the longer your verse. The parents *oooh* and *aaah* and look happy and clap even when somebody forgets what they're supposed to say or just comes on and stands there staring out at everybody without saying a word.

When you're up on the stage you can smell all of the perfume coming together, and I always think that smells more like Easter to me than all of the flowers in the church.

Mother's calling me to go. She's got my robe and head scarf over her arm, all pressed. I don't know why; it's going to get wet anyway.

I put on my old school coat, but then I take it off and put it over my arm. I just can't put it on on Easter Sunday. Mother starts to say something, but she doesn't.

We say happy Easter to Mrs. Beene, who is standing with the cats at her feet. She's wearing a new hat and a pink suit, with the handkerchief I gave her folded with the points showing in the pocket. She starts to smile at us, and I think she starts to say something, but she doesn't; just stoops down and shoos the cats away and goes back inside.

Mother stops in the hall to fasten the hatpin in my grandmother's hat, but I go out to wait for them on the sidewalk, shivering a little because it's not so warm. I start to jump up and down a little to keep warm when I see somebody coming up the street. He is carrying a big bag over his shoulder. He's got long legs and he's walking fast. "Bob!" he calls to me.

I can't move. I can't believe it. Mother sees him and

comes running down the front steps and across the
yard, my robe flying out behind her. She runs up the
sidewalk and throws her arms around the man. He picks
her up and kisses her so hard, her straw hat falls over her
ear. It's my daddy. I stand there like a scarecrow as
Sweetmama goes trotting over, and she just hugs him
and Mother together. Then they remember me. I can't
look up from the sidewalk. I can't. It's too much. Next
I feel my daddy pick me up and I put my head on his
shoulder and hold on to him like a crawfish. He smells
like he always smells. The same since I was a baby. He
has a hard time pulling me loose. I feel embarrassed
and real shy when he puts me down and steps back to
look at me. "You look like an angel in all that pink,"
he says.

Then he comes over and kneels down and tries to
look up in my face, which is facing the sidewalk, and he
pushes my chin up and makes me look in his eyes. I
knew it. Those old bubbly tears just start sitting in my
eyes.

Mother comes and puts her arms around my shoulders. She rubs the chill bumps on my arms. "Bob a big
girl. She's grown up a lot."

Mother talks like that, I begin to cry, and then my
daddy holds his arms open and I just fall right into
them.

After we go back upstairs so Daddy can shave and
change into another sailor suit, he tells us he wasn't
sure he could come until the last minute. "I had to
hitchhike a couple of times," he says, "but I made it."

"We knew he was trying to get here for Easter, Bob," says Mother, "but we didn't want to tell you in case he couldn't make it. You get your hopes up; he couldn't come, be too hard on you."

He tells us he heard the news about Shirley's father, Leon. "It's tough to talk about it now," he says. "I can almost see him sitting across this table throwing back his head, drinking beer."

My daddy gets up and goes over to the sink and takes out his razor. "We'll talk about this later. Now we got to hurry."

Daddy shaves real quick, and we walk to church together. He is holding Mother's hand, and I am holding on to his other sleeve. They keep talking about the war and about the baptizing. I just rub my hand up and down his sleeve and pat his hand once in a while. He says he's got ten days before he has to go back to the war. "One whole day," he says, looking down at me, "you and me, we're going fishing, talk about the world —life, and about that letter you wrote me supposed to be funny."

"I'm ready," I say. "Really ready."

Sweetmama says she's so excited, she's feeling like a Lucky Strike. "First time I smoke on the street," she says, taking off her light blue gloves that match her suit and pulling a cigarette out of her purse. Daddy lights it for her.

"Well, it ain't going to hurt nothin'," she says, taking a big suck on the cigarette, and then she puffs the smoke out in one long sheet. "When this war is over,

I'm never going to look at a cigarette again."

Then she looks over at me. "Hey, Bob," she says with a wink, her cigarette bobbing on her bottom lip, "looks like you got your navy blue and white anyhow, didn't you?"

I look up at my father in his sailor suit. It's so true, I can't say a thing.

ABOUT THE AUTHOR

Barbara Campbell was born in Arkansas and moved to St. Louis, Missouri, at the age of six.

Ms. Campbell was a reporter for *The New York Times* for thirteen years and was nominated for a Pulitzer prize in 1969. Her articles centered on city affairs, civil rights, Black culture, and on social welfare issues relating to the poor, the elderly, and children.

Ms. Campbell lives with her sons, Jonathan and Zachary, in Greenwich Village, New York. She is currently at work on another novel.